P9-ELP-806

THE SCIENCE OF THE X-MEN®

by LINK YACO and KAREN HABER

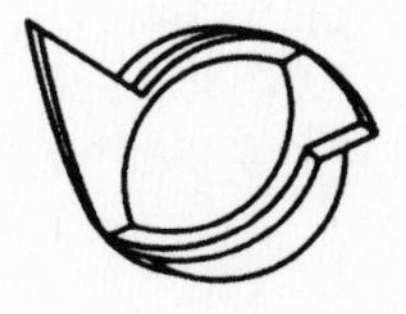

BP BOOKS INC

DISTRIBUTED BY SIMON & SCHUSTER, INC

Special thanks to Mike Thomas, Mike Stewart, Peter Sanderson
and the late Mark Gruenwald.

THE SCIENCE OF THE X-MEN

A BP Books, Inc. Book

PRINTING HISTORY
BP Books, Inc. edition / June 2000

Edited by Dwight Jon Zimmerman.
Cover art and design by Mike Rivilis.
Interior design by Westchester Book.

For information, please write: BP Books, Inc.
24 West 25th Street, New York, New York 10010

The BP Books World Wide Website is
http://www.ibooksinc.com

ISBN 0-7434-002-0-8
PRINTED IN THE UNITED STATES OF AMERICA
10 9 8 7 6 5 4 3 2 1

Shoshke-Rayzl mayner sheyner kluger froy—*Link Yako*

For Len Wein and Chris Claremont—*Karen Haber*

TABLE OF CONTENTS

CONTENTS

INTRODUCTION

All of us are unique. Proof of that is seen in every crowd. Even identical twins—though similar in so many ways—have differences. What you might not realize is that many of us are mutants. Not in big ways. Maybe a freckle or mole that shouldn't be there. A little tuft of hair growing in a funny place on your back. A slight bit of the wrong color in the iris of your left eye, or a patch of hair on your head that's differently colored than the rest. Tiny little mutations like that happen all the time.

The X-Men, and all mutants with super powers, all got good, functional mutations. The reason for this is in the amazing X-genes that all super-powered mutants possess. The X-genes are contained in a section of the human genome fallaciously known as junk DNA because upon its initial discovery scientists could not find anything useful in it. These X-genes were implanted in mankind's prehistoric ancestors by the mysterious, space-faring race known as Celestials. But having X-genes is not the same as displaying power. It takes a separate, mutagenic event to activate the otherwise dormant genes. This mutagenic event can be anything from having parents exposed to radiation (as in the cases of Professor X and Beast), to having a traumatic event during adolescence (as with Cyclops and most other mutants), or some other significant occurance. Also, there is anecdotal evidence that suggests a correlation between the individual mutant's environment (both natural and social) and the type of power manifested.

Scientific method works in four stages: observation, hypothesis, testing, and theory. Only observation results in fact. All else is theory. Newton's theory of gravity, Darwin's theory of evolution, and Einstein's theory of relativity are all theories. They are good, testable theories, but there is always the possibility that something else could come along and replace them. So there are a lot of maybes and probabilities and possibilities with science.

This book is an exploration of those possibilities. Even though the mutant X-genes are found in all the mutants with super-normal powers, it is not the alpha and omega of their powers. Thanks to the Human Genome Project, we've discovered a lot about what makes up the genetic structure of people. As you will see, traits and characteristics are found not just in one gene, or a small group of genes, but can be found all over the DNA strand and in special sequences. When you consider that humans have three billion base pairs of DNA and 100,000 genes distributed in 46 chromosomes, the sequencing possibilities are enormous.

Brains are a lot more complicated that we originally thought, too. There is no single area for most functions. You can't pin down a single memory to a single spot in the brain any more than you can locate the skills for football or basket weaving in any single area. And no one is quite sure if thought is chemical or electrical, although—surprisingly—it seems to be chemical.

We didn't cover every X-Man. There are just too many! We'd have to write another book or . . . two to cover them all. (Say! Now there's an idea!) But you will find many of your favorites including Wolverine, Jean Grey, Professor X, as well as Magneto and some of the other super-villains. We even take a brief look at the alien races of the Shi'ar and the Brood. They may not be mutants, but they have crossed the paths of the X-Men so many times it was impossible not to include them.

The X-Men have been around since John Kennedy was president. Stan Lee and Jack Kirby's concept for a team of genetic mutants was very avant garde. Eventually, technology caught up with their ground-breaking concepts and we are able to use today's scientific knowledge of the concepts of genetics, mutation and evolution to understand the existence of the X-Men. Zoology and anthropology come in handy here, too. We can also use the ideas of physics and quantum mechanics to explain some of their powers. We can even look toward molecular biology to postulate the actual construction of some of the mutant physiologies.

Whoa, that's a lot of science! And an awful lot of different disciplines! It would take a team with as diverse skills as the X-Men themselves to cover all this ground! Fortunately, I've had a lot of help.

What is a scientist anyway? It's hard to find one that will admit to being one. They all call themselves researchers, designers, engineers, teachers . . . anything but a scientist. If we take a look at the original word, *scienta*, which is Latin that came to us English speakers via the Norman French and the Catholic missionaries to what was then a largely pagan England, we see that it simply meant "knowing." A scientist is a specialist in any field of knowledge. Karen Haber, my collaborator on this, backstopped me on all the technical writing. The scientists I am particularly indebted to are my scientific advisors, Matt Stenzel, Ph.D., Dr. Jack Juni, Massachusetts Institute of Technology communications specialist Randall

Winchester, and science writer, Daniel Pendick. They contributed extensive time and efforts. Any scientific errors in the text are my doing, believe me, not theirs! And catch this—Dr. Jack and I went to high school together. I was the liberal arts guy and Jack was the one who built his own ham radio . . . and electric guitar. Now he's a world-famous lecturer on nuclear medicine and a successful inventor.

Matt Stenzel, who has one of the most difficult doctorates around, the math Ph.D., is a pal from my first job after college. I worked at MIT where Matt labored away at degree after degree. For a year or two there, we would hang with the gang at the student pub, the Thirsty Ear, where he would tell us tales of improbable science and I would do my best, in my liberal arts way, to offer tales of improbable scientists. MIT was full of both. Matt is an Assistant Professor of Mathematics at the Ohio State University's Newark campus. He received his Ph.D. in 1990 from MIT. His research area is differential geometry, a branch of mathematics, which, among other things, describes the motion of objects on curved surfaces. His research has appeared in the *Journal of Differential Geometry, Annals of Global Analysis and Geometry*, and the *Journal of Functional Analysis*.

Randy Winchester used to join us at the Thirsty Ear Pub. He is in charge of video transmission and satellite systems at the Massachusetts Institute of Technology, where he has worked since 1982. He has worked on many broadcast firsts, including the first direct to local station live digital audio broadcast in 1984 and early attempts to broadcast video on the Internet. His hobbies include composing microtonal music and gardening. Daniel Pendick is a freelance writer in Brooklyn, NY. His work has appeared in *New Scientist, Astronomy, Earth* and *Scientific American*. He received a Master's degree in the history of science from the University of Wisconsin and was a

Knight Fellow in science journalism at MIT in 1998–99. David Sanders was my continuity advisor. David Sanders, a collector of X-Men comics for over ten years, was a National Science Scholar and a John Jay Scholar and has a B.A. in Archaeology from Columbia University. He has done research and data analysis at the Pupin Physics Labs and the Braeside Observatory. David's comics collection covers the entire X-Universe, making him a living repository for X-Men information and continuity. He created and maintains Mutatis Mutandis, one of the largest and most comprehensive X-Men websites to date. Visit it at http://members.xoom.com/charleyx.

I also got help from a roomful of people: Eliot Juni, Ph.D. (my father-in-law, who has an entire species named after him—I didn't marry into a family, I married into a species!), Rosemary Yaco, Ph.D. (the African doctor), Murray Yaco (who brought divining rods to Vietnam), Ken Horowitz (a serious New York businessman by day, nostalgic X-freak by night, who spent enormous amounts of time reading and critiquing), John Fairstein (working holographer), John Heebink (yet another artist pro, whom I've known since high school), Mike Mosher (ditto), Andy Yaco-Mink-Kalfayan (young man with a computer), Alex Yaco-Kalfayan (younger man with at least one computer, maybe more).

The greatest help of all in the writing and production of this book has come from my wife Susannah. Although she hates science even more than comic books, she is brilliant with computers and endlessly supportive in ways other than purely technical.

PSIONICS

Many of the most important X-Men, including their leader, Professor X, have psionic powers. The term psionic comes from the Greek letter *psi*, which was used as a symbol for unknown quantities in mathematical formulae. A half century ago, Robert H. Thouless, an early researcher in psycho-kinesis, used *psi* as a designation for the paranormal phenomenon he attempted to quantify. In the February 1956 issue of *Astounding Science Fiction/Science Fact*, editor John Campbell combined *psi* with radionics (those electronics related to radio) to create the term psionics.

Psionic power is not just telepathy. It includes any paranormal power and it has come to be especially familiar in reference to powers of the mind. One such power is telekinesis, which is the ability to move matter. What do both telepathy and telekinetics have in common? The ability to control matter.

Thought is not an electrical radio wave. It cannot be "read" with an antenna. Thought is matter. It is mostly neurochemical reactions with some attendant electrical phenomena. Neurochemical reactions can be measured with a number of physical methods and telepathy might be one of them. This would mean that telepathy senses the actions of molecules in neurochemical reactions and replicates them in the brain of the telepathic receiver. This means that psionics might be capable of controlling other physical phenomena, as Storm controls the weather and the Scarlet Witch controls the quantum probabilities that make up what we call luck. And if psionics can manipulate matter at the quantum level, who knows what else they might be capable of?

JEAN GREY

Jean Grey was one of the original members of the X-Men team. She also has one of the most complex histories of the group, an analysis of which could fill a book of its own. Through the course of her long career she has been known by different names including Marvel Girl and Phoenix. To avoid confusion, we'll refer to her here as Jean Grey. Additionally, we'll only be dealing with Jean Grey's powers and not those of the cosmic-powered Phoenix Force.

TELEKINESIS AND TELEPATHY

Jean Grey, whose abilities manifested themselves when she was 12 years old, is a very powerful telepath, perhaps second only to Professor X among the mutants with this ability. She has telekinetic abilities that enable her to levitate and manipulate objects. Her telepathic powers allow her to read minds, project her thoughts into others, and stun the minds of opponents with psionic blasts.

Jean Grey's power of telepathy falls under the heading of extra-sensory perception (ESP). Telepathy refers specifically to the transmission of information from one mind to another, without the use of language, body movements, or any of the known senses. (Clairvoyance, which may be considered a subset of telepathy, refers to the acquisition by a mind or brain of information which is not available to it by the known senses or from any other mind or brain.)

Telepathic-like acts of communication occur in several species. Many insects, such as ants, communicate without touching or producing a sound. As ants wave their antennae while they do this, it was once thought they might be conversing telepathically. Now we know that they are exchanging pheromone-like scents. Other animals manage seemingly soundless communication through body language, or, in the case of whales and dolphins, through sounds that sometimes fall outside our range of hearing.

Aside from some rather dubious research conducted in the former Soviet Union, there have been no documented cases of conclusive extrasensory mental powers in humans.

One of the most infamous examples of the Soviet "research" was the work of Semyon Davidovitch Kirlian and Valentina Kirliana. In 1961, they published a paper in the Russian Journal of Scientific and Applied Photography that described their method of placing an object onto a piece of photographic paper and then passing high voltage through the object. The photographic paper subsequently showed a glowing 'aura' around the object.

Despite their lack of scientific grounding, these "Kirlian Auras" have encouraged the development of pseudoscientific theories regarding invisible auras surrounding living objects and greatly encouraged New Age philosophers in their belief that human thought exists independent of the biochemical systems we call life. But there is really no proof to this effect.

ESP: TELEPATHY AND TELEKINESIS

How can Jean Grey's telepathy function? At least one theory suggests that there could be certain segments of the brain equipped with the physiological equivalents of transmitters and receivers. Tempting though it is to believe that such transmitters' and receivers' functions might be bioelectrical in nature, that theory thus far has not held up under careful examination.

There is, of course, no evidence that Jean's powers are purely electrical. If they were, the electrical field she produced each time she used them would be powerful enough to make every hair on her body stand on end, and to interfere with the operation of any nearby radios, TVs, and computers. What's more, the magnetic field that would be induced—for you can't have an electrical field without inducing a surrounding magnetic field—would attract every paper clip, or other magnetically-sensitive object, in the room.

The electrical fields involved in living beings are extremely weak and, it would seem, more likely the byproduct of the chemical reactions of life, rather than a driving dynamic behind living and mental processes.

ELECTROCHEMICAL NATURE OF THE MIND

The nature of thought is currently considered to be more chemical than electric, so a genetic model that would boost the electrical current of the human mind would not work.

When researchers first measured the speed of nerve impulses, they couldn't understand why reaction times were measured in milliseconds (thousandths of a second) instead of picoseconds (millionths of a second) which should have been the case if nerve impulses were electricity, for electricity travels at the speed of light.

The current thinking (no pun intended) is that nerve impulses are actually a cascade of minute neurochemical reactions. No electrical current travels through the nerves. Rather, a wave of reactions courses along its lengths. It is like the waves on the ocean—the water stays still but the waves travel through it. Electrical impulses are generated by the neurochemical reactions, and this is why for so long it was thought that nerve impulses were electrical. Thought is nerve impulse in the brain. Here too, these impulses are chemical reactions that only incidentally generate electricity. When brain waves are monitored with an electroencephalogram (EEG), these electrical waves are reflections of chemical processes.

The brain is not a circuit board with electrical impulses moving from one transistor-like neuron to the next. When a neuron, the basic component of a nerve, receives a chemical signal, it releases a small electrical signal along the dendrites, the trailing tentacle-like ends of a neuron. These in turn stimulate more chemical releases which flood across a gap called the synapse and stick to the dendrites of the next neuron.

There is, however, some question as to which comes first—the chicken or the egg. A minority of researchers considers that there is a possibility that it is the electrical transmission that causes the chemical reactions, not vice versa.

In any event, the electrical fields produced are very

weak—weaker than that generated by a single triple-A battery. They are not nearly strong enough to power an electric light bulb, let alone levitate an object into the air.

If Jean's powers were electrical in nature, the field she produced would be powerful enough to interfere with the operation of the electronic gear and communications devices that the X-Men routinely utilize. But not a one of them has ever uttered a peep about all the static, screen noise, or system crashes Jean has been causing.

TINKERING WITH BASIC FORCES

There are four basic forces in nature. Electromagnetism is one. Gravity is another. The strong and weak nuclear, or binding, forces of the subatomic realm are the final two. As with Iceman (whom we'll be discussing later), perhaps Jean is able to affect gravity or the binding forces to move objects.

Jean Grey might be able to directly apprehend and manipulate the chemical interactions in the brains of others, controlling their very actions and thoughts. Taking this a step further, Jean's telekinetic powers could be the result of chemical reactions generated by certain mutated segments of her brain that set up corresponding chemical reactions in other external locations.

Telekinesis refers to the power of the mind to manipulate matter at a distance without any known physical means. Although little proof exists currently for confirmation of this power, there are a few dramatic demonstrations of such paranormal abilities as levitation, which have never been explained in accepted scientific terms nor disproved. Perhaps in the case of the mutant X-Men and Women, and

Jean Grey in particular, altered brain structures have resulted in unusual extra sensory powers and perceptions.

MICRO-BLACK HOLES

A lot of the X-Men seem to have access to power that a regular flesh and blood body couldn't generate. As with Cyclops, Jean might be able to employ organic cold fusion to produce micro-black holes that open a gateway into a non-Einsteinian universe where physical laws as we know them do not apply.

To open a hole into another universe requires an enormous amount of mass compacted into a very small area. In astronomy, such black holes result when stars burn out and collapse into spheres millions of times smaller than their original form. This produces enough weight to punch a hole in the very fabric of the universe. Scientists theorize that the center of our galaxy contains one monster of a black hole.

Normally, it takes a mass equal to three times the size of our sun to initiate a gravitational collapse and produce a black hole, or what physicists and mathematicians call a "singularity" because of its singularly unique properties in our time-space continuum.

Stephen Hawking first discussed micro-black holes. Hawking suggested that special conditions, such as spinning, might make any size of black hole possible. The significant factor is not the original amount of mass, but the amount of compression. However, it would take unique circumstances to create micro-black holes.

Jean cannot actually carry a micro-black hole in her head. The gravitational forces generated by such phenomena would squash her to bits—although in her subjective experience, as she approached the event horizon of the black hole, time would dilate and her death would take a very . . . long . . . time. Nevertheless, this might be the doorway to her source of power.

If Jean Grey had her own personal doorway into another dimension and/or universe, it would certainly be a convenient means of accessing exotic powers. How the controlling mechanism to such a doorway would work is another question (see the entry on Professor X for more on this). Obviously, whatever the control is, it must prevent her from being destroyed or sucked into that alternate reality.

So far, no one has ever come up with a way to even theoretically control a singularity. We will discuss the possibility of cascading chain reactions at the quantum level in the Iceman entry. Shortly (in about two paragraphs) we'll broaden that cascade approach to include strong and weak nuclear forces. Maybe some combination of these could conceivably do the trick.

NEURONS, SYNAPSES AND WEAK FORCE CASCADES

Jean's ability to read and influence other people's thoughts suggests an ability to directly apprehend and manipulate the chemical and electrical interactions of the neurons in the human mind. If we use the logical tool of Occam's Razor, which states that one should never look for a complicated explanation when a simple one would do, and look for an explanation that will fit both her telekinetic powers as well as her telepathic ones, we are led to conjecture a physical intervention in her subjects' minds, using the same physical powers described above. To control another's thoughts would imply directing chemical activity. Perhaps she uses, instinctively, her telekinetic ability on a molecular level. To read their minds, she might be able to manipulate her own brain's activity, by lock stepping it with her subject. If she can direct her power to such a microscopic degree, perhaps she can lock in on her subject's brain activity and make her own synapses fire in parallel, thus mirroring their thoughts (for more on this see the Professor X entry).

The information must be transmitted through some unique method. There's an awful lot of information involved so any simple radio frequency transmission would have to be either very broadband or heavily compressed and encoded. In either case, there's been no evidence of radio wave activity during her telepathic exchanges. Nor do lightning storms—or even passing trucks with powerful CB radios—interfere with her telepathic performance, as one would expect if it were a radio-based transmission.

Since we've been considering the utilization of strong and weak nuclear forces, we should look at how these too could be used for transmission. Although these forces normally function only at the quantum mechanical level, they do have effects that lead all the way up to our own human-sized reality. In fact, they hold matter together.

Here we're going to consider cascading chain reactions of the effects of the strong and weak nuclear forces. Perhaps Jean can effect a resonance in matter across a distance in this fashion.

This might be how Jean's psionic powers allow her to affect physical matter. When this is applied to larger objects, it manifests as telekinesis. When she applies her power to the subatomic working of the neurochemicals in the human mind, her power manifests as telepathy. Just as she can exercise her telekinesis on any object, she can exercise her telepathy on any mind. Other telepathic mutants can use their powers to counter hers and block the effect. Or they can use their powers in concert with hers to effect two-way communication. When Jean and Professor X converse telepathically, they would manipulate the neurochemicals that make up thought in each other, to produce the communication they desire. And when they both hurl their powers at a foe, they could either direct separate telekinetic control cascades or combine them, focussing their powers on the same enemy brain, and coordinating their attack telepathically with each other.

QUANTUM INSEPARABILITY

There is also another way that to create "spooky action-at-a-distance effects". There is a phenomenon called quantum inseparability. The Einstein-Rosen-Podolsky Effect and Bell's Theorem both state that any quantum particles which once influenced each other continue to influence each other no matter how far apart in space and time they might move afterward. These particles are said to be in "entangled states." This system of communication only works for two people with the ability to manipulate quantum particles, and it is a limited system that only produces simple messages—which can act as encryption keys. It is, however, absolutely practical and not too far out of reach of present technology.

Think of a completely secure communications system—an encryption-system—that lets you send coded messages that no one can decode. That's what the most practical application of this principle would achieve.

Let's posit a quantum communication system where the receiver, whom we'll call Professor X, receives a message from the sender, whom we'll call Jean.

Professor X reads a message from two physical bits. But Jean has sent only one transmitted bit, which means that Professor X keeps one reference bit in his possession at all times.

Professor X has two photons, or two spin-half particles, that are both in an entangled state. He stores one particle and sends the other to Jean, who stores it.

Both particles must be isolated from their surroundings to make certain the entanglement is maintained.

When it's time to send a message, Jean does one of four operations on her particle, using either spin-half particles or photons. With the spin-half particles, these four operations are no change, or rotate the spin by 180 degrees around three axes, x, y or z. With photons, the polarization can also be rotated.

Then she sends her particle back to Professor X.

These operations, although performed only on one particle, affect the entangled quantum state of both particles.

Complicated laws of quantum physics demand that the Professor cannot detect which state his particle is in until he has the other to compare it with. Once he's got it, he can decide which of the four operations Jean performed, and therefore, receive one of the four messages, and respond accordingly.

Should anyone else intercept the particle that Jean's sending it would be of no use to them, because they would need the Professor's "receptor" particle to translate the information.

To perform this theoretically possible communication, we have to assume that we will soon be able to build two theoretically possible devices. One is a "quantum gate" which performs what is sometimes called a Bell measurement that allows us to compare two quantum particles and determine their state. The other device would have to let us easily alter that state. Right now, these are beyond our technological capabilities. However, there have been optical experiments that are the first steps in this direction.

BRAIN DEVELOPMENT AND FUNCTION

Telepathy is not, evidently, something that is simply that is simply turned on or off. It is a trait that one may possess to varying degrees. Someone can be just a little bit telepathic like Mastermind or enormously telepathic like Jean Grey and Professor X. Different orders of telepathic power seem to utilize different parts of the brain.

Human brains come in three parts that we have retained stages in our evolutionary development. We have the brainstem, which we inherited from our reptilian ancestors, the cerebellum, which is a more recent mammalian addition and the latest evolutionary upgrade: the cerebral cortex, or frontal lobes, which are particularly well-developed in humans.

Nature is a lazy designer. Organisms retain bits and piece of earlier evolutionary stages. Our appendix and tonsils, for instance, are largely useless, but we retain them from our distant ancestors. A closely observed embryonic development will reveal a fetus going through stages where there is growth of a vestigial tail and even gills.

In the same fashion, we retain the original lizard's brain stem. This intellectual organ has remained largely unchanged for hundreds of millions of years. Our brain stems are nearly indistinguishable from those of monkeys and not very different from those of iguanas. It remains quite separate from the more recent developments of the cerebellum, which is common to all mammals, and the cerebral cortex, which is uniquely developed in modern humans.

The brain stem performs brain functions for which we don't need the higher powers of a full-fledged cerebellum or cortex. Anger and fear come from this level. All other emotional responses, such as love, or fascination, also originate here.

So, the emotions might be stimulated by the modern forebrain but they are generated by the hindbrain. In fact, the hindbrain may be responsible for our instinctive emotional reactions to situations and people.

These instinctive responses are even more basic than emotions. You wouldn't even have to be a telepath to "read" this level of response in another person. Expert poker players and politicians can disguise their instinctive responses but those of us in the audience struggle to mask our basic reactions. It stands to reason that this kind of basic "thinking" would be easily read even by a weak telepath, and just as easily stimulated.

On the next level up is the mid-brain, or cerebellum. This is a brain that we have in common with all mammals. Thanks to the cerebellum it is possible to be "dead on your feet" from fatigue, or a dazing blow, and still be able to perform simple tasks. For this reason, a prizefighter, essentially unconscious after receiving a number of punishing blows, can continue to throw punches. This would be a good area to target if a telepath wanted to evoke sleepwalking or a similar behavior in their subject and not have their victim realize it. Under this sort of control, a subject might be manipulated to pocket secret plans and later dump them in a blind mail drop, all without knowing what he or she had done.

The final layer of the brain is the mostly recently evolved

part, the cerebral cortex. Thought functions in many ways in the cortex. This is where speech occurs. Most likely, advanced telepaths would concentrate on this area in order to read the articulated ideation that issues from the speech center in the cortex.

Mathematics, music, and visual skills come largely from a part of the cortex called the visual cortex. This is an older part of the cortex and not a part of the brain that deals with elements of conscious reasoning.

Language, identity, and self-awareness come from much newer parts of the mind than do math skills. Many animals perform what amount to vastly complicated mathematical calculations: when a cat measures how far it must jump and at what angle to land precisely on a three-inch window ledge, it is actively performing calculations, not simply relying on a static bank of acquired experience or hard-wired genetic responses. Neurologist Oliver Sacks dramatically explained this in his clever and fascinating case studies (several films have been made from his writings, including *Awakenings* and *Regarding Henry*).

EINSTEIN'S BRAIN

Einstein didn't have a heavier head than you or me. Recent evidence suggests, however, that he lacked a section of his brain called the parietal operculum, which allowed a larger development of other parts of his brain. His inferior parietal lobe was 15 percent wider than normal because a groove that typically runs through the parietal area of the brain developed in a different direction than is usual. That groove, the Sylvian fissure, was hardly there at all. It usually divides the inferior parietal region, but in Einstein's case, the area was relatively continuous. This is in a region, as is the visual cortex, which processes dimensional visualization, spatial relationships, and mathematics, as well as other operations. Other areas of his brain were slightly smaller and his mother often told the stories of how he was slow to learn to speak when he was an infant.

Perhaps mutants actually have likewise altered structure in their brains. It might be that by taking in a few tucks, as with Einstein's brain, other structures could be enlarged and utilized more effectively.

TYPES OF THOUGHT

Thought can be memory, which can involve conjuring up recollections of any of the five senses. As everyone's memories differ, and have vastly different connotative emotional values, interpreting the memories of another person might prove quite a challenge to a telepath.

Thought can be visual, musical, or mathematical. If one were to read another person's visualization processes, he might find it difficult to make sense of the process on a conscious level, as the visualization areas do not use the symbols of speech or conscious thought.

Thought can be verbal. Sometimes we actually think in words and even sub-vocalize these words. Sub-vocalization is an unconscious and inaudible voicing of speech where the larynx goes through the motions of speech but little or no air is forced through the vocal chords to produce audible sound. This sort of extremely self-conscious thought is largely generated by the speech center of the brain and might be easier for a telepath to read, or at least make sense of, than other types of thought. However, speech involves many different parts of the brain, not merely the speech center. It can simultaneously draw on memory areas, math areas, etc.

There are many other kinds of thought. No one has developed a definitive list of such types and such a list might not be possible. Any combination of any type of thought is possible as well. The thought processes of the human mind are hugely complex and perhaps limitless. However, although a human mind does generate great complexity, it can also comprehend it, and a mutant mind might have unique structures that equip it to make sense of such intricacies.

The human mind is immensely complex. When its neurons fire chemical discharges across its synapses in the process of thought, it opens up at least one universe of possibilities. It has been estimated that there are more possible combinations of synaptic firings than there are electrons in the universe. That's a huge amount of possible thought. And it appears even more awesome when one considers that each person's mind is filled with different memories, so the combinations of synaptic firings have a different result. Add to that, the fact that all brains vary somewhat in construction, and some persons, like Einstein, have great differences.

COPYING MINDS

It is theoretically possible to create a copy of a person's mind. You could write down all the compositions of all the neurons. It might one day be possible to physically analyze and describe all the memories that are chemically encoded into the cells of the convolutions of the brain.

Or you could record it on computer memory media. The

way things are going we could get that down to the size of a human head. We might even be able to encode that information into pure energy waveforms, such as exist in the vacuum of space. But just recording the brain doesn't make for a functioning brain. The chemical functions of synaptic firing are biological in nature. To get waveforms to interact as if they were a pile of sticky organic cells would be quite a trick.

PROFESSOR X

Professor Charles Xavier is the founder of the X-Men and perhaps the most potent telepath in the world. He is regarded as one of the most highly regarded authorities on genetic mutations. Not only can he read and project thoughts, he can control the actions of others. Xavier can maintain limited control over a group of people or complete control of one person, if he is within that person's physical presence. He can project his astral form for limited distances or greater distances on "astral planes" where he can create "ectoplasmic" objects. He has Ph.D.s in genetics, biophysics and psychology, and qualifies as a genius by whatever criteria you'd care to apply.

ELECTROMAGNETIC WAVES

It's possible that Professor X's psionic powers radiate like radio frequencies. Radio waves are, of course, electromagnetic waves and therefore consist of magnetic and electric fields that vibrate at right angles to each other at the same frequency. Other rays belonging to the electromagnetic group include radar, infrared, ultraviolet, and X-rays. All electromagnetic waves move at the speed of light, 186,000 miles per second.

It's possible for radio waves to travel harmlessly right through the human brain. (In fact, right now, even as you read this, there are all sorts of detectable radio broadcasts from all points on the RF spectrum going right through your brain.) Then what about transmitting "thought waves" from brain to brain?

Thought produces low voltage current. Low voltage/low frequency radio broadcasts can go great distances. Of course, the minimum voltage requirements for conventional radio frequency broadcasts are several orders of magnitude greater than what the normal human mind can generate. But we're talking about a mutant mind here, not a normal one. And, possibly, this particular mutant mind produces an exotic form of energy that can not only span considerable distances but affect the workings of other minds as well. A mutant mind might be able to generate much higher voltage. Of course, this would have detectable side effects, such as interfering with television reception.

Like all waves, radio waves have a particular frequency or wavelength. Frequency is a measure of the number of waves transmitted per seconds, measured in hertz. Wavelength is the measure in meters of the length of each complete wave.

The original sound signal is superimposed onto a radio wave, modulated so that the wave carries the sound. This is the modulated wavelength that radio transmitters broadcast. Modulated radio waves are sent through an amplifier that in turn delivers the waves to a transmitter.

What if Professor X's brain not only functions as a modulator and transmitter, but as an amplifier as well, sending out powerful thought waves at a specific "frequency" that humans and mutants are equipped to receive?

In case you're worried about Professor X's brain being able to take the strain of all that energy, consider this: Electro-Convulsive Therapy (ECT) delivers a brief shock of about .5 amps at 90 volts, or about 50 watts, and regardless of the debatable effectiveness or potential harm of the procedure, the majority of patients survive it. Evidently the neurons of the brain are reasonably durable and can handle a fair amount of voltage. And we're not even talking about a mutant brain here.

One of the higher frequencies for brain wave activity is Beta activity. This is called "fast" activity. Wave frequencies are measured in hertz (Hz), named after the German physicists Heinrich Hertz, and wave motion is defined as the number of complete oscillations or cycles per second. Beta activity has a frequency of 14+ Hz, and is the normal major rhythm in people who are alert or anxious . . . or just have their eyes open.

Beta frequencies don't broadcast at all that we know of—certainly not any detectable distance. However, the frequency range of Beta waves overlaps with the frequency range of ELF, so it is conceivable that with adequate power and a long enough antenna, Beta waves could broadcast.

It is true that astronomers are developing ever more sophisticated means, with both software and hardware, to detect radio signals from stellar distances (see Brood entry). Perhaps the psionic members of the X-Men already possess the physiological equivalents of the hardware—and software—needed to transmit thought.

STRING THEORY AND ELF

According to string theory, all matter vibrates, but in a multi-dimensional manner. Superstrings are a way of looking at particles as one point in a multi-dimensional string that vibrates at different rates. This is one possible way psionic frequencies could transmit.

When electricity has no frequency, it is considered simply Direct Current (DC) such as is provided by batteries. Beta frequency almost qualifies as DC It doesn't even qualify as a radio frequency: the lowest radio band on frequency spectrum, Extremely Low Frequency (ELF), is at just a slightly higher frequency, 30–300 Hz.

ELF can go through solid rock and oceans. It broadcasts for thousands of miles. If mutant brains can produce a frequency about twice the rate of normal, they could radiate in the ELF range. And the already great range of ELF might be further extended with amplitude modulation.

There are two methods of broadcasting: Amplitude Modulation (AM) and Frequency Modulation (FM). AM can bounce off cloud layers and ping pong between earth and sky to great distances. But even if you use AM methods, the results are very iffy because they depend a lot on weather conditions.

Perhaps mutant psionic activity transmits at a slightly higher range than normal Beta rhythms, up in the ELF range. Maybe with a little amplitude modulation that range could be extended even further.

ELF broadcasts work with very low voltages but require very large antennae, a minimum of 90 feet in length, to accommodate the extra long waves. Coiled antennae can be used to receive longer wavelengths—imagine the "meat" equivalent residing in a mutant brain.

As we said earlier, thought is more chemical than electric but electrical impulse is a detectable byproduct of thought and might be used to indicate it for communication purposes, just as, while speech itself is not electric, radio waves can transmit it.

Of course, it is also possible that mutant minds might very well be generating exotic forms of energy. There are a number of possible origins for these energies including manipulation of the binding properties of the weak nuclear force of the subatomic world, energy from a non-Einsteinian universe, organic cold fusion, and spinning micro-black holes.

PSYCHONS AND THOUGHT

A thought particle, dubbed a "psychon," was theorized by Sir John Eccles, a renowned neurobiologist and Nobel Prize winner. Sir John's theory goes something like this: concepts, memories, and thoughts are stored in the brain as synaptic connections in the dendrites, the neuron extensions that receive input.

According to Sir John, whenever the brain is activated in thought, stimulating these synaptic connections (dendrons), it produces a psychon, an elementary particle. The theory here is that the psychon is a thought unit and consciousness then arises from psychon interactions. If, indeed, this is the case, then is Professor X emitting powerful psychons that travel great distances to affect the minds of his targets?

HILBERT SPACE AND ECTOPLASM

Essentially, Professor X has the same telepathic powers as Jean Grey, but to a far greater degree. One major difference between them is his ability to operate on an "astral plane" and create "ectoplasmic" objects. Let's substitute the term "dimensional" for astral, and consider something called "Hilbert Space."

The idea that there are other planes of existence is hardly new. Almost a century ago, German mathematician David Hilbert defined the mathematics of multi-dimensional time-space, giving rise to the term "Hilbert Space" for infinite dimensional space.

Modern physical theories of the universe, particularly string theory, postulate up to twelve dimensions, of which we non-mutant humans normally perceive three and a half: length, width, height, and a portion of time.

Given the concept of infinite, multidimensional "Hilbert" space the possibility exists for all theoretical alternative universes including those (non-Einsteinian, of course) in which mutant powers might originate.

Professor X's astral plane projections might take him on an infinite dimensional journey. If mutant telepaths can detect and manipulate exotic energy in three-space (our universe), why not through infinite dimensional space as well? And perhaps that exotic energy, whatever it might be, is visible in infinite dimensional space and is what the Professor perceives as ectoplasm.

In Edwin Abbot's *Flatland*, written about a century ago, he fictionalizes the life of theoretical two-dimensional life. When a three-dimensional creature (like us) invades the flat, 2-D universe, it seems to appear out of nowhere. A 3-D finger poking into a 2-D plane appears as a point that expands to a larger circle.

Similarly, a multi-dimensional creature, poking its infinite dimensional finger into our 3-D world, would appear first as a small sphere that grew larger as it passed through our plane.

Professor X's astral plane might be an infinite dimensional journey. As for a fish out of water, the view from infinite dimensional space would appear distorted and disorienting. Short distances in infinite dimensional space could be great distances in three-space.

If mutant telepaths can detect and manipulate exotic energy in three-space, why not infinite dimensional space as well? And perhaps that exotic energy, whatever it might be, is visible in infinite dimensional space, just as other space-time distortions, such as alternate universes, might be. This might be what the Professor perceives as ectoplasm. It's all a matter of perspective.

When Professor X extends his psionic powers into Hilbert Space, he might not be actually leaving his body. As the mind is a neurochemical construct, it can't leave the body without the physical brain leaving the body too. But perceptions can certainly leave the body. It would be like a virtual reality experience. He would perceive and feel all the sensations of Hilbert Space even though his body hadn't entered that space. Only his psionic powers of telepathy and telekinesis would enter that infinitely dimensional realm. And there, he would be just as vulnerable to psionic attacks as if he were actually there. If, as we have suggested, psionic powers are actually a cascade of subatomic quantum particle chain reactions, any psionic barrage could travel the psionic path back to his physical body, tracing the chain of quantum cascades to their source. One might say that his "astral self" is illusory, but then, our normal physical perceptions of self are—in a sense—illusory as well. We depend on our senses to build a picture of reality. Color, for instance, does not actually exist. It is just an arbitrary designation attached to a certain bandwidth of light frequency.

Hilbert did his work almost a century ago and since then there have been a few developments that have suggested that although the entirety of the space-time continuum or multiverse has infinite dimensionality, our particular universe has only a dozen. Mostly, in the past decade, the theorists have come up with some complicating factors. What they think is that the universe is constructed of about a dozen dimensions. The first four are fully expanded but the next eight are curled up to unimaginably small levels.

So if the other dimensions are all squirreled away, getting at them might be even more complicated then we've already supposed. It might be that a dimension traveler would have to twist himself up in the same way the higher dimensions are twisted. It might involve reduction in size!

That Professor X has been able to think "small" enough to breach the dimensional barrier, and has done it many times, is a compliment for his ability to micromanage his thoughts.

MASTERMIND

Jason Wyngarde was a mutant with delusions of grandeur. Unlike normal humans who could only dream of being strong, handsome and irresistible to the opposite sex, he was able to live his fantasy. In reality he was of average height, slender build, plain features, and an arrogant, pusillanimous personality. In the fantasy his mutant ability allowed him to project he was tall, well-built, handsome, dashing and debonair.

Mastermind was a member of Magneto's Brotherhood of Evil Mutants and later other secret mutant organizations that sought world conquest. But the one conquest that Mastermind sought above all else was that of the heart. Mastermind was attracted to beautiful women, among them Scarlet Witch and Jean Grey. They in turn were all repulsed by him—that is to say, the real him. When he created the dashing fantasy image of himself, he was irresistible. Invariably, though, the fiction collapsed, and he was rejected and left even more bitter than before.

It was only after he died after contracting the fatal Legacy Virus that it was discovered that he had had sufficient success with one woman to sire a child, for a woman claiming to be his daughter, and who also possesses his power, has made herself known.

TELEPATHIC IMAGERY

Mastermind generated detailed, realistic illusions that were convincing to almost everyone. He had psionic powers that could manipulate the five senses of other people and make them see, hear, touch, smell, and taste things which just aren't there. What's more, he could alter the appearance of objects, including himself, or make them seem to disappear altogether.

His illusions could not be recorded on film, tape, disk, or any other storage media. He did not project holographic images. His power was telepathic or psionic.

His illusions were so authentic in appearance that most people couldn't help but feel, even if only on a subconscious level, that they were real. If he created the illusion of a solid object, most people, despite their awareness that the object isn't real, still won't be able to force their hands through it.

HUMAN PERCEPTION AND MISPERCEPTION

Illusions are essentially misapprehensions of reality. Our minds are constantly striving to make sense of the information our senses receive. The wonder isn't that we sometimes get it wrong, but that we get it right most of the time.

It isn't that difficult to deliberately confuse the senses and create illusions. Magicians and filmmakers do it for a living. But they're not alone. The fine art of illusion making is practiced by lawyers, politicians, advertisers, and even experts in psychological warfare.

There are many ways to induce illusions. Let's begin by considering the techniques and/or syndromes that result in effects that most resemble some of Mastermind's telepathic manipulations.

FOLIE A DEUX

One person with delusions can influence another to share them and they don't need psionic mutant powers to do it. "Folie a Deux," literally "the folly/craziness of two," occurs when one person establishes a strong emotional affinity with another and in the process passes along his or her delusions.

Mastermind might have done this psionically, but a delusional person can do it via an emotional bond. Mastermind might have stimulated the hind brain of his victim to achieve that bond—once his victim felt emotionally linked to him, he or she would willingly take any hint of a suggestion from Mastermind.

Clinically speaking, there are three features to this psychotic disorder:

1. A person or persons has/have an already-established delusion and a delusion develops in another individual in the context of a close relationship with the first person or group of persons. This can happen in a family unit or with an artificial extended family such as a religious cult.

2. The delusions of the second person might not be identical but are similar to those of the first delusional person.

3. There are indeed psychotic aspects to "Folie a Deux" but other psychotic disorders such as schizophrenia or a mood disorder do not account for this disturbance. Neither can it be directly attributable to physiological effects of illegal drugs, prescribed medication, or a general medical condition.

STOCKHOLM SYNDROME

Similar to "Folie a Deux," this disorder was named after a hostage situation in Stockholm, Sweden in 1973 where four hostages were taken during a botched bank robbery. Six days later, the hostages actively resisted rescue, refused to testify against their captors once they were released, and raised money for their captors' legal defense.

One of the hostages became so emotionally attached to one of the robbers that she broke off her engagement to another man, became engaged to her captor, and remained faithful to him during his prison term. In this syndrome, hostages take the viewpoint of their abductors. The strong psychological instinct to survive promotes a tendency of victims to identify with their oppressors in an effort to gain their sympathy.

Once the captor has established a powerful bond with his victims, he is remarkably influential over their psyche. Not only will they take his point of view, they will augment and support it. This appears to be a form of brainwashing. Certainly Mastermind would not have hesitated to allow his victims' minds to do most of the work for him.

HYPNOSIS

Hypnosis is somewhat like sleep but researchers have found that the brain wave patterns of hypnotized subjects are more like the patterns of deep relaxation. Hypnosis is generally considered to be a type of receptive, highly focused concentration where outside or unnecessary events are disregarded.

No final definition or explanation has ever been developed for hypnosis. The British Medical Association and the American Medical Association define it, in part, as "a temporary condition of altered attention in the subject that may be induced by another person." Exactly how that temporary condition is induced is the question. Mastermind might have been exactly this state but with more direct means than a normal non-mutant must use.

Trance Induction and Termination Hypnosis are achieved basically by inducing deep relaxation and focused concentration. Subjects become very unresponsive to normal stimuli. They are told to sleep but they are also told to listen and be ready to do whatever the hypnotist says. No research has definitively established what part of the brain is stimulated in a hypnotic state. It might be the sleep centers or some part of the brain stem that control muscular and metabolic relaxation. If this is the case, Mastermind would have had an easier job of controlling his victims, bypassing contact with the exponentially more complicated midbrain or forebrain entirely.

When the subjects believe that they are asleep, they are less critical than they would be if normally awake. In this state they will accept orders or ideas from the hypnotist, even if the ideas are extreme and/or eccentric. However, hypnotic victims have shown resistance to taking immoral or illegal actions. Therefore, if Mastermind used a form of hypnosis, he would have to make his victims think whatever they were doing was morally acceptable.

The usual hypnotic techniques are simple. Hypnotists can

use direct commands or monotonous suggestions repeated over and over, to place their subjects in a trance-like state.

Subjects might be asked to stare at a moving object, concentrate on some repetitive sound, or focus on the hypnotist's voice. The hypnotist tells the subject over and over again to breathe deeply and comfortably, feel drowsy or relaxed, let their eyelids grow heavy and close, and go into a deep sleep. Telling subjects that something simple, such as opening their eyes, is impossible tests the depth of the trance. Then they invite subjects to try it.

Depending on the subject, it can take a few seconds or a few minutes to achieve trance. Once that occurs, suggestions can be made by the hypnotist that will induce hypnosis in the subject again later at an agreed upon signal. The results of this signal can be instantaneous.

People in a hypnotic trance are very suggestible. Although they are able to walk, talk, speak, respond to questions, and otherwise perform normal actions, their perceptions can be drastically influenced by outside suggestion. For example, a hypnotist can make subjects ignore pain, sweat and change their heartbeat and body temperature. A hypnotist can also make subjects relive the past as if it were the present, recover forgotten memories, or have hallucinations. What's more, when the "fun" is over, the hypnotist can command the subject to forget all or part of the hypnosis session.

Post-hypnotic suggestions can also be made to which the subject will respond at a later time by means of a specified signal or trigger. When this happens, on signal, a subject will resume his or her hypnotic state, perhaps for a short period of time, thereby altering certain behaviors. Some specialists use this technique as a therapeutic means to help cure headaches, severe itching, and anxiety attacks.

At the end of a supervised hypnosis session, subjects are usually wakened at the command of the hypnotist who tells them to return to their normal state and to feel well and alert. Nevertheless, some subjects may feel disoriented and drowsy for some time afterward.

The more thoroughly the subject believes in the power of the hypnotist, the more easily they can be hypnotized. A hypnotist should have some authority in the view of the subject. It's easier for an "expert" or a psychiatrist to hypnotize than for some average cluck. That would have worked to the advantage of Mastermind, who had a bit of a reputation.

A good hypnotic subject is imaginative, intelligent, calm, and interested in new experiences. That would certainly apply to the X-Men. Genetic predisposition might also be a partial factor. Between 20 and 30 percent of the population can be deeply hypnotized. Some research indicates that only 5 to 10 percent can be hypnotized deeply enough to experience visual hallucinations and about 10 percent of adults cannot be hypnotized to any degree. Mastermind seemed to achieve a far greater percentage of effectiveness.

TACTILE AND AUDITORY ILLUSIONS

Mastermind proved capable of enhancing the impressions of illusions that occur naturally. These illusions were occasioned by normal functions of the mind, often where our expectations affect our perceptions. For example, if you hold a large softcover book in one hand and a small hardbound in the other, even though the two books weigh exactly the same, the larger one will feel lighter.

If you hold one pencil with your fingers crossed, it may feel like two.

If cold water is poured over one hand and hot water over the other, then both are stuck into lukewarm water, the cold hand will feel very warm and the hot one will feel cold.

If you hear two sounds, one after the other, the volume of the second is compared with the first, so a regular speaking voice can sound like a yell in a room full of whispering people, or a speed metal concert can make everything else inaudible.

All of the above examples have been manipulated in one way or another by Mastermind.

VISUAL ILLUSIONS

Let's now look at the naturally-occurring visual illusions Mastermind could manipulate.

Color and Brightness Contrasts: If you look at a blue surface right after staring at an orange one, the blue surface will look much brighter. This is because they are "complementary" colors, opposite each other on the color wheel, and the color receptors of the retina take a moment to refresh after sensing a color. Until they do, they are more sensitive to the opposite, or "complementary" color.

Closure: The psychological phenomenon of closure makes a viewer perceive the motion on a video or computer screen as continuous instead of a series of still pictures shown at sixty per second—or 24 frames per second in the case of film. The same phenomenon makes a person unconsciously complete or close an incomplete visual image such as a square or a triangle missing a side. The eye normally continuously refreshes the image it perceives and distinguishes the differences that indicate motion. This is a natural instance of closure.

With film and television, motion is more artificially portrayed. The eye can distinguish motion far faster than visual media can record. That is why wagon wheels in film westerns or car wheels in TV commercials sometimes appear to be going backwards—the film is missing some of the images that would convince the eye that actual movement is being portrayed.

Try freeze-framing a fistfight on your VCR and you'll see the fighter's limbs are blurred, although you may not perceive that when the tape is running. With these media, the brain must supply the missing image information and infer the movement.

This is made a bit easier by the phenomenon of persistence of vision. The eye retains afterimages of what we see as it refreshes the optical chemicals in the retina. These afterimages can help fill in the gap between frames in film projection, where there is a split second of blackness between frames, and video, where there is also a split second of blank screen while the electron gun swings back up to the top of the screen to begin tracing the new image on the phosphors of the screen.

Illusionists can therefore rely on their subjects assisting them via closure. Mastermind might only have had to give a few psychological cues to his victims and nudge their minds to fill in the rest.

Figure-And-Ground: This is also known as "object reversibility." An illustration of a white vase against a black background can also look like two black profiles framed in silhouette against a white background. This effect also works with the Necker cube, a set of lines that looks like a symmetrical drawing of a transparent cube that seems to tilt up or down depending on how you view it. (Chronological note: Younger people generally see the cube's flip-flops more easily than older folks do.)

Perspective: This makes distant objects appear smaller than near ones and can cause illusions. That's why the moon looks larger when it's near the horizon. Hollywood filmmakers take advantage of this phenomenon to make their sets appear bigger than they really are. They build objects—such as furniture or houses—smaller at the back of a set to appear farther away. In one film, midgets were even used at the back of the crowd to achieve the same effect.

Convergence and Divergence: In what is known as the Ponzo Illusion, one circle touches converging lines, and another equal circle is between the lines where they are farther apart. The first one appears larger even though it's exactly the same as the other. This is probably because the converging lines trigger our perspective mechanisms. Linear perspective creates the illusion that parallel lines, such as railroad tracks, come closer and closer to each other as they recede from the viewer.

Vertical and unbroken lines seem longer than horizontal and broken lines. A drawing of a hat that is really no taller than the width of its brim appears taller than it is wide. This is because we tend to see vertical lines as longer than horizontal, and probably stems from an evolutionary need to condense our horizontal sight. If saber-toothed predators might be lurking out beyond the cave's mouth, our ancestors would have needed to receive and assess all the really important visual information as quickly as possible.

Humans also have a tendency to see a broken or intercepted line as shorter than an unbroken one. Again, our brains are trying to condense information for analysis. An unbroken line needs less analysis.

Mirages: These are the result of atmospheric refraction of light. For example, driving along a straight two-lane road on a hot day, the pavement ahead of you may appear to shimmer, even to contain puddles of water which disappear as your approach.

Refraction or bending of light can alter and break up an image. However, this wasn't part of Mastermind's modus operandi. He used psionic powers to mess with people's heads. But since we're talking about different kinds of illusions, let's consider the different sorts of mirages, just so we know what kind of things Mastermind *couldn't* do.

Inferior mirage: these appear as rippling pools. When dense cool layers of air refract the sun's rays at one set of angles and warmer, thinner layers of air refract at different angles and they create a shimmering effect that looks like water. This is how the mirage of a pool of water can appear in a desert, or along that road we were discussing. The illusionary water is actually the reflected image of the sky above.

Superior mirages: These are caused by layers of cool, dense air some distance above the surface of a body of water. The image gets inverted when it goes through this inversion layer. A ship can appear to sail upside down above the horizon. Below this inverted image the real ship can usually be seen unless it is out of sight below the horizon.

Fata Morgana: This is the most fantastic mirage of all, named for the legendary sorceress Morgan le Fay, and is seen over the Strait of Messina between Italy and Sicily. During this mirage, fantastic castles arise from the sea and change their shape. A combination of superior and inferior images probably form it. Layers of air change, distort, and magnify the image of the cliffs and houses on the opposite shore. The houses may appear as turreted castles. Similar mirages in other places are also called Fata Morgana.

Quivering images and heat devils: Look through the heated air above the flame of a match. Objects will be distorted. This is caused by the unevenly heated air rising, acting as prisms and distorting the light rays reflected by the objects. "Heat devils" are often seen in wide expanses of open country and "heat waves" are seen over hot radiators. They are the results of the same phenomenon.

MASTERMIND'S M.O.

How did he do it? Like Rogue (whom we'll encounter a little later on), Mastermind simulated natural phenomenon with unnatural means. His power was psionic, as is that of Rogue, Jean Grey, Professor X, and Storm. As we have seen, illusions can be caused by a wide variety of methods that affect many different parts of the brain. Mastermind was indeed a master of the mind for he seemed to be able to control all these diversified methods. As with most mutants, his power was probably instinctive. When he produced fear or love in his subjects, it was doubtful that he was consciously stimulating the hind brain. When he produced visual hallucinations, he probably didn't know that he was stimulating the visual cortex, increasing the secretion of serotonin, etc. He was not interested in science but, rather, in effects.

The pity of Mastermind was that the fantasy his power allowed him to create magnified the failure of his real life.

STORM

Ororo Munroe can control weather. She can cause the precipitation of moisture in any form, generate wind and rain, create storms and lightning and even discharge these electrical charges from her hands. She can also fly. She utilizes the wind to carry herself aloft in a form of gliding. Ororo's mother was a princess of a tribe from Kenya. Ororo's father was David Munroe, an American photojournalist. While her family was living in Cairo, Egypt, her parents were killed in a terrorist attack when she was a child. She grew up an orphan and learned how to survive using her wits in the streets of Cairo. Much later she traveled to Kenya and it was there, in the shadow of Mount Kilimanjaro that her power over the weather manifested itself. It was there that she became the protective "goddess" to the local villagers.

This peaceful life changed when, one day Professor Xavier visited her, told her about the origin of her power and about his team of X-Men, and asked that she join them. After some thought, she accepted his offer and has been a member of the team ever since.

POWERS OF WEATHER CONTROL

Storm's weather-manipulating ability is psionic, and with it she can cause precipitation of moisture in any form, raise or lower temperature and humidity, generate storms of considerable intensity, and create electrical atmospheric phenomena. She can also discharge lightning from her bare hands.

While she can manipulate weather patterns, she can't completely alter them, nor can she create atmospheric conditions that can't exist naturally. For example, she can't lower temperatures as far as absolute zero or raise them to solar intensities.

The weather in Storm's immediate vicinity changes with her emotions. Dark clouds can gather overhead if she's unhappy. (Remember those lightning bolts!) Storm makes every effort to keep here motions under control, but she's not always successful.

Her powers can be very specifically localized, to the point where she can create a mini-storm to water a potted plant. In addition, she can create atmospheric effects in a beam-like path radiating from her hand. Her control over the atmosphere is so specific and tightly focused that while creating storms over a large region she can select smaller areas within the storm radius and shield them from her own cyclones.

The mutant X-genes that form the basis of all mutants with super powers appears heavily influenced by emotional and/or psychological state of each mutant. Storm was claustrophobic and living in a rural, natural setting where she felt safe for the first time since early childhood. The open sky and the forces of nature were a psychological focal point for her. It might be more than a coincidence that when her powers manifested, they too focused on the open sky and natural forces. It might also be noted that circumstantial evidence suggests that the raw material available to young mutants seems to affect the nature of their powers. Storm didn't have metal around her, as Magneto, Jean Grey and Professor X did. She had a natural setting, and that became the focus of her power.

For Storm to affect weather and cause a wide variety of meteorological phenomena, she must be able to affect air movement, humidity, particulate matter in the atmosphere, and many other factors. One tool at her disposal is the control of wind.

Storm utilizes the wind to carry herself aloft in a form of flight that resembles gliding. She has also used wind to deflect physical attacks. When she's aloft, Storm can literally travel as fast as the wind, and has reached speeds up to 300 miles per hour. Her body automatically adjusts itself to the surrounding temperature although there's a limit to the stress her body can withstand from such changes.

METEOROLOGICAL CHANGES

Storm produces meteorological effects in seconds. Her psionic abilities allow her to telekinetically move masses of air and moisture. Telekinetic manipulation of atoms and molecules could also heat and electrically charge these masses. Storm's application of psionic forces is different than those of other mutants and requires a specialized understanding of how weather works. For example, Professor X and Jean Grey probably couldn't create a thunderstorm. Though they have strong psionic abilities, they wouldn't know what they needed to apply their powers to. Storm's understanding of the weather seems to be instinctive. Perhaps her unconscious telekinetic probing of meteorological forces has given her this understanding. Or perhaps this information was hard-wired into her genes.

METEOROLOGY

Meteorology is the study of weather. Weather is extremely complex and caused by many factors. As with most sciences, there are a lot of conflicting theories. Some meteorologists say that the movement of the air is the most important factor to consider. Others say that air movement is caused by uneven solar heating, and that *that* is the main event. Some of the other factors to consider are humidity, precipitation, particulate matter, electrical charges, and cloud cover.

For Storm to affect weather and cause a wide variety of meteorological phenomena, she must be able to affect many or all of these factors. One tool at her disposal is the control of wind.

The atmosphere is in constant motion. When air sinks, we have good clear weather and the air is stable. When air rises, it is unstable and cloudy and murky weather. By generating heat or cold, Storm could cause air to rise or fall. This might imply that she can create cold as Iceman does, which further implies a psionic origin to his power.

Air blows in response to differences in atmospheric pressure and that once air begins to move, the Coriolis force, a physical phenomenon, tends to bend it to the right of its intended path in the Northern Hemisphere and to the left in the Southern Hemisphere.

Wind motions can have a variety of effects on the environment. Wind can make waves in the ocean, which sounds innocent enough, but storm waves can be as tall as buildings and have the force of a large bomb. Wind can also move soil and shaping sand dunes, which, at its most extreme, can turn farmland into a dessert in a few years.

Much weather phenomena is produced at frontal boundaries between air masses. Thunderstorms, tornadoes, and hurricanes are the most extreme examples of this.

All these atmospheric factors would probably not change, if it weren't for some very basic physical relationships between the Earth and Sun. These relationships cause uneven heating of the Earth's surface. The Sun doesn't directly heat the air. The atmosphere is actually heated by the Earth's surface.

Weather changes occur daily. The difference in day-and night-time temperatures is a factor. Weather also changes seasonally because the Earth tilts when it revolves around the sun so that different parts of the globe are always being heated at different times.

Even without considering the axial tilt, the amount of radiation that is absorbed by the Earth is affected by several factors. The Sun's radiation hits the spherical Earth at different places at different angles. The sun is closest at the equator and there the planet gets the full solar dose. North and south of the equator, the surface of the planet curves away from the Sun and things get cooler.

The planet's rotation around the Sun is another factor. The orbit of the Earth is not a perfect circle and the speed of our path around the Sun is not always exactly the same. Gravitational pull from other planets in the solar system affects our orbit, even if only slightly.

Heated air expands and cold air contracts. The density of the air increases the force it has to press down on the Earth's surface. This force is measured as air pressure, which has an average of 15 pounds per square inch (psi). Cold air has high pressure (because the air molecules are closer together, making the air heavier) and warm air has low pressure (because the air molecules are farther apart, making the air lighter).

Density and temperature of air generally lessen with height, so the higher you are physically, the less air pressure there will be. However, even at the highest reaches of the atmosphere, in the exosphere, where there is hardly any air, let alone air pressure, there are phenomena associated with the weather.

Not only do air movement and solar heat affect weather but also various gases in the air, which are part of natural chemical and organic cycles. Atmospheric moisture is also a factor. The transformation of water from the gaseous to the liquid or solid state is an important source of energy in many meteorological processes. Clouds can absorb huge amounts of heat and so they are a big factor as well.

Changing any one of the many factors that cause weather can create meteorological events. "Seeding" clouds with particulate matter can force them to condense their moisture into rain. Storm might telekinetically move dust into a cloud formation and trigger rainfall.

Much weather phenomena is produced at frontal boundaries between air masses. Thunderstorms, tornadoes, and hurricanes are the most extreme examples of this.

Some meteorologists have considered destroying hurricanes with a drastic change in internal pressure, dropping bombs into the "eyes," or centers of the hurricanes. Storm could use the same technique by creating pressure or removing it via telekinetic manipulation of air masses.

Storm moves masses of dust by means of telekinesis, "seeding" clouds and triggering rainfall. It's reasonable to assume that she not only alters the kinetic power of the winds and temperature of the air and water, but affects the density of air layers and the electrical charge of cloud masses as well. This is one mutant you want on your side when you're planning a picnic.

SCARLET WITCH

Though more known as a member of the Super Hero team the Avengers, Wanda Maximoff is a mutant. She is the daughter of Magneto and the sister of Quicksilver. She and her brother initially encounted the X-Men when they were members of their father's original Brotherhood of Evil Mutants, one of the X-Men's earliest foes. She and her brother later left the Brotherhood of Evil Mutants to join the Avengers. Quicksilver soon left the team, but the Scarlet Witch remained and, except for some brief periods, has remained with the Avengers.

The Scarlet Witch has probability-altering power, which she sometimes manifests as "hex-bolts." By a combination of gestures and mental concentration she manipulates chaos energies to create hex-spheres, small pockets of psionically-induced reality-affecting power that causes a disruption at the molecular level of probability around her target. In other words, she makes improbable phenomena occur.

She has effected disturbance of energy fields and signals, spontaneous combustion of flammable objects, rapid decay and rust of inorganic and organic materials, abrupt melting of gun barrels, poltergeist-like deflection of flying objects, and rapid removal of air from a given area. These events happen almost immediately after she finishes her hex.

The field's range is limited by her line of sight. She cannot affect something she reads online or in a newspaper, or sees on a CD-ROM, video or even live television.

Her hex-casting ability is unreliable about 20% of the time and much of it depends a lot on her physical condition. When she is exhausted, hung over, or has the flu, she has a tough time casting a series of hex-spheres quickly. Normally she can do this and get desirable results for almost an hour. However, she can't can't levitate, shoot magical energy concussive blasts, or transmute elements. The Scarlet Witch possesses limited magical abilities, which mainly serve to enhance her mutant power's reliability, but due to her training under the sorceress Agatha Harkness, she has the unrealized potential to be a very powerful sorceress.

MANIPULATING CHANCE

In a sense, we are all bred for luck, and have lucky genes. Chance plays a role in all events and in evolution as well. How large that role is remains a matter for discussion. Controversial evolutionary theory pundit Stephen Jay Gould believes that chance plays an enormous role in evolution, and that it was extremely unlikely that intelligence and humans should evolve. Many academics disagree: they think it was inevitable that we would evolve as we did.

However large a role chance does play in evolution, it is inarguably a factor to some extent. And so, to that extent, we can say that "lucky" people survive, and if, indeed, there are genes for luck, we have been developing them for a few hundred thousand years. So, in addition to possessing X-genes, the Scarlet Witch possesses a higher than average amount of these luck genes.

Her own ability seems to be influenced by probability and is therefore unreliable. Probability, as the eminent theoretical physicist Erwin Schrödinger (1887–1961) would be among the first to tell you, is a funny thing. The early state of quantum mechanics theory in physics seemed to imply that you could alter the outcome of an event merely by observing it. It is possible that she has the ability to influence events on a quantum level via some heightened electromagnetic sensibility. More on that later. It is also possible that she is able to influence the movement of objects through a combination of telepathy and telekinetics.

Take, for example, melting a gun-barrel. This event would seem to imply that the Scarlet Witch has created a field in which the molecules that make up the metal of the gun are so excited that they heat to the temperature at which they can no longer remain solid. A further implication here is the use of electromagnetic force to influence the movement of the molecules in the metal. It certainly argues for the use of some form of telekinesis. In all likelihood, the Scarlet Witch has composite powers, an interwoven array of telekinetic and telepathic abilities which have combined in her to affect objects on the molecular and even subatomic level. The main thing the Scarlet Witch does is congealing probability into actual phenomena.

LUCK AND CHAOS THEORY

Luck, or probability, is a phenomenon that has been intensively studied by mathematicians. If you flip a penny heads or tails enough times, a number of patterns occur. One obvious pattern is that, provided one does so often enough to establish a statistically reliable pattern, it lands heads up half the time. But other patterns show up as well. Statistical clumping is one. The heads will not be evenly distributed throughout the coin-flipping—one out of every two tosses won't be heads—so there will be periods when there are either a prevalence or lack of heads showing up. The distribution of these periods is a matter of some analysis. Theorists have carefully charted seemingly random distributions. The results of those analyses represent a broad spectrum of opinion. This is to say, no one agrees on what chaos really means.

Chaos theorists think there is pattern in seeming chaos. The main thing about chaos theorists is that they have shown how apparently simple deterministic laws or processes may drive random behavior.

The game of roulette shows the difference between random and chaotic systems: The gaming statistics show that the sequence of numbers is completely random. That's why Einstein said, "The only way to win money in roulette is to steal it from the bank." However, the mechanics of the ball and the wheel are well understood. If you can manage to perfectly measure the initial conditions for the mechanical roulette system—weight and mass of materials, strength of the spin, and so on—you could make a short term prediction of where the ball will land when the wheel is spun. Given this notion, it's surprising that the Scarlet Witch hasn't gone to Las Vegas to make her fortune at the gaming tables.

DETERMINISM

Some believe that if we truly knew *all* the variables to a situation, and had the brains or computing power to process it all, we wouldn't regard anything as random. It's like the philosophic concept of determinism that was so popular in the 19th century. Determinists, among them Samuel Clemens (aka Mark Twain), believed that if you really knew all the factors in a person's life, there was no such thing as free choice. We don't decide to become brain surgeons, plumbers, or Super Heroes because of conscious rational choice. Rather, we are driven to these results by the genes we were born with, the way we were raised, the moral systems instilled in us by both, and maybe just our mood at the time we made the choice.

CLASSICAL NEWTONIAN MODELS

Aficionados of classical mechanics heavily endorsed the deterministic model. Followers of Newton believed that it's not enough just to know how something changes in time; you have to know how it starts out.

To use classical mechanics to make predictions you need to be able to know the configuration of your system at some instant in time. This "initial condition" cannot be measured to perfect accuracy, and it is an unfortunate fact of life that small inaccuracies in the initial conditions may evolve into enormous errors in the predictions after some finite amount of time. That's one of the reasons why weather prediction doesn't work too well over time periods longer than five days.

But that doesn't by any means imply that the classical model of the world is entirely screwy.

For example Newton's equation F=ma (*F*orce equal *m*ass times *a*cceleration) is pretty helpful. It is a model that makes testable predictions about the motion of macroscopic objects, such as planets and orbiting satellites, and these predictions turn out to be very accurate and useful in many situations. They even got several astronauts to the moon!

But the classical belief that you could just figure out everything and the outcome would be inevitable is naive by the standards of today's science. We will *never* be in a position to know *everything* about a situation, let alone have the processing power to evaluate it, so we will never know if just how random things really are.

THE PARADOX OF THE CAT IN THE BOX

As far as we're concerned, an awful lot of the universe is random. Small particles of matter vibrate randomly. This was observed by Robert Brown (1773–1858) about 150 years ago, and dubbed "Brownian" motion. Randomness is particularly apparent in physics at the quantum level, where Erwin Schrödinger had a lot of fun with it, much to the later irritation of Albert Einstein.

For the sake of example, Schrödinger devised a metaphor for quantum mechanics of the "Cat-in-the-box." In his scenario, someone has dropped a cyanide capsule into a box containing a cat, and the odds are equal that the capsule will or will not break.

In the actual world, the cat would have an equal chance of being alive or dead. But in the quantum world, until the box is opened, the cat exists in a "mixed state," neither alive nor dead, awaiting the determination of its fate when the box is opened. Schrödinger's implication here (and paradox) was that as soon as the scientist observer looks at them, the electrons decide where they are. In other words, observation affects outcome.

Einstein didn't buy it for a second. But that is the famous paradox of Schrödinger's Cat.

If we apply Schrödinger's Paradox to the Scarlet Witch's powers, we may say that she affects events by looking at them on a quantum level and telling all those electrons decide exactly where they want to be.

The point of quantum mechanics for the Scarlet Witch is that all matter is in a fluctuating state of probability until you pin it down with observation. What the Scarlet Witch seems to do is influence that flux of chance and extend it beyond the quantum level all the way up to our size. If the odds are a hundred to one that a super-villain will trip over his shoelaces (or Velcro-tabs, depending on his footwear) at a crucial moment, the Scarlet Witch tips the odds so the villain definitely loses the footwear "bet."

So then, we have to wonder exactly how she does that. If the role of the observer is indeed important to the way probability shakes out, then she might simply have the ability to observe on a quantum level, with some heightened electromagnetic sensibility. If she can nudge a particle here or there via telekinesis, so much the better for affecting the outcome of events.

OBSERVING QUANTUM CASCADES

Nuclear Magnetic Resonance Imaging, (NMRI) examines a person's body by heightening the magnetic field of the patient's tissue and photographing by X-Ray the differences in the charges which show as lighter or darker on the NMRI film. Although an NMRI deals with matter on a much larger scale than the quantum level, a similar technology is used to examine subatomic structures.

What if a person were to be able to directly perceive those subatomic structures and their differences? Further, what if Schrödinger was right? That person's perceptions might actually shape probabilities at the quantum level. It might require an awful lot of "quantum peeping" to affect things on our level, but then again, maybe there is a cascading effect, like shooting one pool ball and setting an entire pool table into motion.

Most people, by the way, can actually directly observe some quantum-level events. A fully dark-adapted eye can perceive as little as one single photon of light. Then imagine that single photon of light reflecting off the Scarlet Witch and striking our fully dark-adapted eye. And if that happened the way we wanted, then wouldn't *we* be the lucky one!

EXOTIC POWERS

Many of the X-Men have powers that seem to defy the laws of physics. They have access to incredible amounts of energy and that energy is of a completely unknown type. It is like nothing in this universe... and that is the key to understanding what science could lie behind it.

Ours is very possibly not the only universe. We do know that it hasn't always been here. It appeared about 12 billion years ago. And it probably won't always be here. Theoreticians predict a heat-death of our universe perhaps in 40 billion years from now, depending on how much dark matter there is between the stars.

What will always be here is the multiverse—the infinitely dimension fabric of reality. Our universe probably consists of only 12 dimensions. In the other dimension might be held any amount of universes. And the laws of science could be very different there. But how to get there? Some physicists believe that the immense black holes at the center of most galaxies are already opening portals to other dimensional space. Stephen J. Hawking thinks that spinning black holes might allow reasonably safe passage through the fabric of the universe.

But using black holes, even spinning ones, would be worse than having a tiger by the tail. How would you control such immense physical forces? For decades, researchers have tried to control plasma fusion with powerful magnetic fields but they have had only limited results. But the psionic control evidenced by mutants such as Jean Grey and Professor X might have an application that would allow access to vast resources of powers. If you want to know exactly how this might work and precisely what powers they could harness . . . read on!

MAGNETO

Erik Magnus Lehnsherr, the father of Quicksilver and the Scarlet Witch, is a complex character whose life has been defined by his constant struggle with his own concepts of morality. His values have led him along villainous paths, most notably as the leader of the Brotherhood of Evil Mutants and as leader for the sinister Acolytes, as a martyr, as when he allowed himself to be placed on trial for crimes against humanity, and as a hero working side by side with the X-Men.

As a boy, he saw his entire family murdered by Nazis. He survived the Auschwitz concentration camp. Afterward, when his powers matured and he became aware of his identity as a mutant, he feared that mutants like him would one day be persecuted as the Jewish people were. At times he has wavered between violent enforcement of mutant superiority over normal humanity, coexistence with Homo sapiens, and the creation of a separate homeland for mutants. What has not changed is his belief that mutants, whom he named Homo superior, will become the dominant life form on the planet.

MAGNETIC FIELD MANIPULATION

Magneto can shape and manipulate magnetic fields. He also seems to generate them but possibly draws and collects magnetic particles from great distances. There are two possible explanations for the source of his power, psionic or physiological.

Magneto once lifted a cargo freighter weighing 30,000 tons fifty feet into the air from a distance of 300 feet. He can deflect asteroids. And his powers have multiple simultaneous applications. Magneto has an innate ability to sense nearby metal and can erect magnetic force fields with which to protect himself. These fields are effectively impenetrable.

Although his primary power is magnetism, he seems to be able to manipulate or project other forms of energy related to magnetism. This has enabled him to fire bolts of electricity and to generate heat intense enough to melt a metal door. Most likely he did this with infrared radiation, a part of the electromagnetic spectrum which also includes visible light, radio waves, ultraviolet light, gamma rays, and x-rays. Presumably, he can control any of these forces as well but at considerable physiological cost to himself.

ELECTROMAGNETISM AND ITS SOURCES

It's believed possible that *all* magnetic fields are caused by electric currents. If that's so, then Magneto is obviously producing powerful electrical effects that in turn generate his magnetic powers. He may, in fact, be functioning as a living transformer, increasing or decreasing electrical fields that, in turn, influence magnetic fields. According to Michael Faraday (1791–1867), although a steady magnetic field produces no electricity, a changing magnetic field can produce an electric current. This principle, dubbed "Electromagnetic Induction," is known today as Faraday's Law. What Faraday's Law of induction tells us is that a changing magnetic field induces an electric current. However, with remarkable symmetry, the exact inverse of Faraday's Law is also true: a changing electric field gives rise to a magnetic field. This discovery was made by the great physicist James Clerk Maxwell (1831–1879). What this means is that Magneto may have it both ways: he may be inducing electricity by varying magnetic charges, and may also be generating magnetic power by varying his own electrical fields and those around him.

As with many of the X-Men, Magneto can generate large amounts of energy. But while Professor X produces psionic energy, and Cyclops and Havok generate exotic energies that may originate in another universe, and Iceman generates energy that cools matter drastically, the energy that Magneto produces falls within the standard electromagnetic spectrum.

All living creatures generate some amount of EM energy. For example, we generate heat with our metabolic processes and even minute amounts of electricity with our nervous systems. Magneto generates considerably more—fantastically more energy than normal creatures.

There are two possible sources of his energy. Perhaps, like Storm, his powers are actually psionic and telekinetic in nature. By telekinetically manipulating atoms and molecules, he could polarize them, producing magnetism. Or perhaps, like Cyclops and Havok, he accesses energy from a remote source and channel its magnetic forces.

The electromagnetic spectrum, which encompasses everything from matter to electricity to light and beyond, is so named because all matter is built of electrical energy. With electrical energy comes a magnetic field, and vice versa. In other words, if you have electricity, you can make a magnet, and if you make a magnet, you have electricity. Therefore, it's no surprise that Magneto can control electricity as well as magnetism.

THE SEARCH FOR MAGNETIC PARTICLES

Just as electrons are bundles of electric charges, scientific theory has it that magnetic charges should have their own personal particles, dubbed "monopoles." Physicists have been searching for monopoles for some time without success. However, if these particles do exist, they would be a great source of power and undoubtedly critical to Magneto's manipulation of magnetic fields.

MAGNETISM AND MAGNETIC FIELDS

Magnetism and electricity are closely related. This relationship wasn't discovered until the 19th century. But the history of magnetism begins much earlier, in Asia Minor, in a region known as Magnesia, where ancient residents saw that certain rocks attracted each other. These rocks were named after the region in which they were found, hence the term "magnets."

Only iron and a few other materials such as cobalt and nickel demonstrate considerable magnetic effects and are said to be ferromagnetic (from the Latin word *ferrum* for iron).

Just as we can imagine electric fields surrounding an electric charge so can we imagine that magnetic fields surround magnets. A demonstration of this can be seen when iron filings are placed near a magnet: they will align themselves in a pattern following the magnetic field lines, revealing the shape of the field. The forces between like and unlike poles of a magnet are similar to the forces between positive and negative electric charges: "unlikes" attract while "likes" repel.

Although we can isolate positive and negative charges, we can't cut a magnet in half and thereby isolate its negative and positive poles. By cutting a magnet in half we would have two magnets, each with its own negative and positive pole. This happens because ordinary magnets are made up of many microscopic magnets.

When viewed under an electron microscope, samples of magnetic materials reveal regions known as "domains" which are at most 1mm in length or width. Each domain behaves exactly like a tiny magnet with north and south poles.

In an un-magnetized piece of iron, these domains are arranged randomly so the magnetic effects of the domains cancel each other out. But in a magnet, the domains are aligned in one direction. They may even rotate slightly, and may be responsible for causing a slight alignment of the domains in un-magnetized objects. This, in turn, may account for the attraction between magnets and un-magnetized objects such as the way in which a magnet can pick up a paper clip or metal filing. So may Magneto influence the alignment of domains in objects, drawing them to him or repelling them by psionic means.

POLARIZATION

As previously noted, Magneto may control magnetic fields through psionic telekinetic powers on the subatomic level, aligning particles to produce an effect similar to polarization. Since light rays are electromagnetic waves (in the Einsteinian universe), their energy consists of vibrating electric and magnetic fields. In normal light rays, these fields vibrate in planes at random angles. In polarized light, all the rays are forced to vibrate in the same plane, which is the plane in which the electrical field vibrates. However, Magneto is utilizing more than light rays. Therefore, it may be possible that he is in fact polarizing all particles with a magnetic charge—i.e. all particles—and forcing them to vibrate in the same plane, and to behave as he commands. In this manner he can control all matter.

UNIFIED FIELD THEORY

Physicists theorize that, during the early stages of the formation of the universe—the Big Bang—energy levels were so high that *all* forces were unified. Hence, the Unified Field Theory. On rare and extreme exertions of his power, Magneto has appeared to be able to control all of the four forces of the universe: a one-man unified field. If this is indeed the case, then he justly deserves to be regarded as the most feared and powerful mutant on Earth.

CYCLOPS

Scott Summers was the first mutant to be recruited into the X-Men by Professor Charles Xavier. As Cyclops, he became the first leader of the original team composed of Angel, Beast, Iceman and Marvel Girl (Jean Grey). Cyclops has been a strong dependable member of the X-Men, having served as leader of the team for years during various changes in its membership. He is currently married to Jean Grey.

Cyclops' power first appeared at puberty and, as is coincidentally often the case with mutants containing X-genes, under a crisis circumstance. The adolescent Scott Summers and his younger brother Alex (who later became the X-Man Havok) and their mother, Katherine Anne, were passengers in their father Alex's vintage private plane when it was attacked by a scout ship of the extragalactic Shi'ar Empire (see Shi'ar entry for more about this alien race). In a desperate attempt to save their sons from being captured or killed, Katherine Anne gave Scott and Alex the only parachute on the plane and pushed them out. Overburdened, and as a result of the attack, in flames, the parachute could not support the boys.

Scott was staring down at the oncoming ground when his eyes suddenly emitted energy blasts that softened the ground and sufficiently cushioned the boys' landing to save their lives.

Unfortunately, the landing was not soft enough to prevent both boys from being injured. Scott in particular suffered a head injury that proved to have irreparably damaged the part of his brain that controlled his newly-manifested power. As a result, Cyclops' optic blast power is permanently "stuck" in the "on" position. The only two ways he can dampen his optic blasts are by closing his eyes or by wearing a visor—wraparound glasses or goggles made of ruby quartz. The ruby quartz diffuses the optic energy and renders it harmless and undetectable.

OPTIC BLAST PROPERTIES

Before we explore the possible makeup of Cyclops' optic blasts, let's look at what they can do.

Cyclops can focus the width of his force blasts with his eyes. The depth of his eye-blasts is controlled by his visor's adjustable slit. His narrowest beam, about the diameter of a pencil, at a distance of four feet, has a force of approximately 17 pounds per square inch (psi) or two psi above the standard 15 psi of air pressure at sea level. One of the most powerful eye-blasts he has produced was a beam four feet across which had a force of approximately 500 psi at a distance of 50 feet. One of his broadest beams was approximately 90 feet and had a force of approximately 10 psi across at a distance of 50 feet. The beam's effective range is approximately 2,000 feet, at which point a one-inch beam will spread out to 10 feet square, and then has a pressure of 0.38 psi.

At maximum force, his optic beams can tip over a full 5,000-gallon tanker truck at a distance of 20 feet, or puncture a one-inch carbon steel plate from a distance of 2 feet.

Cyclops also possesses the ability to compute trigometric and geometric relations with great accuracy, like an experienced pool player. This lets him bounce his blasts with considerable precision.

ENERGY TRANSFORMATION AND HIGHER PHYSICS

The energy that comes out of Cyclops' eyes is unusual, to say the least. It generates no heat, no radiation and no electrical or magnetic fields. Although it's visible it doesn't seem to be part of the electromagnetic spectrum. It can manipulate molecules and it has concussive shock power.

Cyclops' first use of his power offers us a clue about the possible nature of his optic blast power beam. Obviously it simply cannot be any form of ordinary energy such as a laser or particle beam. Those forms of energy would merely have burned the ground. There has to be a telekinetic aspect to Cyclops's power because when his beam struck the ground immediately below his brother and himself, it rearranged the very molecules of the ground in order to soften their landing. In effect it acted as a psychokinetic projection of Scott's mental desire for self-preservation.

Let's take a moment to give some background on energy, force and how they're measured.

Kinetic energy is just what is says it is: energy, not force. And yes, there is a difference. In the scientific sense, a force must fit the definition of the four universal forces: electromagnetism, gravity, strong and weak nuclear forces.

By definition, there are only two kinds of energy: kinetic and potential. Kinetic energy is a combination of weight and motion. Momentum and inertia play major roles in kinetic energy.

Scientists use a number of different terms to measure energy including ergs, electron volts, foot-pounds, BTUs (British thermal units), calories and joules. The two that concern us most here are calories and joules. Calories are used to measure energy changes caused by chemical reactions, and joules measure other kinds of energy changes. It takes one calorie of energy to raise the temperature of one gram of water by one degree Celsius. One calorie is equal to 4.184 joules. One joule is the amount of energy needed to lift one pound about nine inches. And so, by inference, it's obvious that a whole lot of joules—and calories—would be required by Cyclops to do the work of generating his kinetic eye beams. (More on calories and joules in a moment.)

Energy is the capacity for doing work. Work is simply moving matter, but that can result in many forms of energy that you wouldn't expect to come out of simple movement. The Law of Conservation of Matter and Energy ($m=E/C^2$) says that energy can only change its form, it cannot be created or destroyed. So, if energy is the ability or capacity to do work, then power is the flow of energy from one form to another over time. For example, in the process of baking a potato, complex starchy carbohydrates are broken down—by heat—to simpler, more easily digested carbohydrates. In this manner, heat becomes chemical energy. (By the way, when we think of calories as food measurement, we're really discussing potential energy measurement. Food contains potential chemical energy that is converted by our bodies to do work by means of kinetic energy.)

The level of the kinetic energy of an object, and how much work it can do, depends upon its mass and velocity. For example, if a truck weighs ten tons and is moving at

70 miles per hour, it has an awful lot more kinetic energy than a kid does on a bicycle.

At the atomic level, thermal energy is the kinetic energy of the molecules in an object. Warm bath water has enough molecular motion to heat it up to a comfortable temperature for humans. That motion is the kinetic energy of the water. Conversely, if the molecules slow down enough, the bath water would freeze. The average kinetic energy of the atoms or molecules of a body is measured by the temperature of the body. To further illustrate, a piece of buttered toast contains about 315,000 joules of energy. With the same amount of energy you could:

Light a 60 watt light bulb for 90 minutes
Nap for 90 minutes
Take a power walk for 15 minutes
Jog for six minutes
Bike for 10 minutes
Drive a car at 50 miles per hour for seven seconds

MATTER INTO ENERGY

It takes only a small amount of matter to create a great amount of energy—as in an atomic reaction—but that transformation, obviously, produces too much heat for a non-mutant human body to handle. If it could be contained, for instance, the way plasma fusion reactors use huge magnetic "bottles" to contain plasma for nuclear fusion reactions, it could be the "motivating force" (if we may use that term) to propel molecular matter.

We can easily conclude that there is no fissile aspect to Cyclops' power. There is no evidence suggesting that Cyclops' physiology is as impervious as an atomic energy plant's containment vessel. In fact, he is vulnerable to everything that a normal non-mutant human is, with two exceptions. He is impervious to the impact of one of his own optic beams, should it rebound onto him. Nor is he affected by the power blasts of his brother Havok. Since for all practical purposes he seems to be composed of normal flesh and blood, something else must protect his body. If he is capable of projecting these energies, he must also be capable of generating a field of some energy within his own body that repels or, more likely, absorbs them.

Havok's energy is different than Cyclops'. Havok's blasts are plasma blasts. Plasma is the fourth state of matter-super-heated gas, stripped of electrons, as occurs in the ionized trail of lightning or inside the giant nuclear reactor that is the sun. This is unusual matter, rarely seen on Earth, but not "exotic" matter, as we will explain.

Evidence suggests a link between sunlight and Cyclops' power. It is possible that Cyclops metabolizes sunlight as a power source for his force beams. The relationship of solar and electrical energy to his power would suggest that his blasts are electromagnetic (EM) in nature but this is misleading. Although they are part of the same spectrum, light and electricity are very different in two aspects.

Electricity is conveyed by the negatively charged subatomic particles called electrons. These are fundamental particles or elementary particles.

Light is another story. The simplest way to explain this is to say that it is composed of quanta packets. Quanta are the plural of quantum, which is vaguely defined as "the smallest amount of energy a system can gain or lose." Quanta are smaller than atoms, and there are a lot of theories as to their exact nature.

The low end of the light spectrum begins with infrared rays, which most living creatures can't see, but some can sense, and progresses through the visible spectrum and then up to the invisible ultraviolet. Above ultraviolet frequencies, we stop calling it light and start calling it radiation. X-rays start happening at this range. At the high-end of the X-ray range is gamma radiation.

Gamma rays come from the sun and the stars, which are gigantic ongoing nuclear reactions. Those few gamma rays that slip through the Earth's defensive shield of atmosphere can cause genetic mutation. We'll get back to radiation particles in a moment.

RUBY QUARTZ

Why can ruby quartz stop Cyclops' optic blasts? The similarity of the red color of the quartz and the red color of his blasts would suggest that his blasts are some form of light, but again, as we have already established, this is misleading as light is part of the electromagnetic spectrum.

By the way, Ruby quartz is not the same as a gemstone ruby—a transparent red variety of corundum—nor synthetic rubies made from aluminum oxide. Ruby quartz is mostly silicon. The red pigment is caused by ferromagnetic metallic impurities in the silicon crystal structure of the quartz. Metallic impurities in silicon and germanium crystals can cause them to have very different properties as semiconductors in computer chips. Essentially, the impurities simply either add free electrons or create electron deficiencies in the crystal structures.

The similarity between the color of the quartz and the color of the Cyclopean blasts would suggest that these blasts are some form of light. For the sake of argument, let's go ahead and assume that there may indeed be some unusual form of light which is a component of the energy emanating from Cyclops's eyes. If so, then the means by which his visors block his blasts could be a process similar to polarization.

In the Einsteinian universe, light rays are electromagnetic waves. Their energy consists of vibrating electric and magnetic fields. In normal light rays, these fields vibrate in planes at random angles. In polarized light, all the rays are forced to vibrate in the same plane, which is the plane in which the electrical field vibrates.

Polarizing filters block all rays except those vibrating in a certain plane. If polarized light strikes a filter whose plane is at right angles to the plane of the rays, no light passes at all. (Polarizing sunglasses work this way. Reflected light is partly polarized and sunglasses—polarizing filters—block that polarized light, reducing glare.)

Does the ruby quartz in Cyclops' visor function like a pair of really powerful sunglasses? It's possible. Quartz is a crystal, and some crystals can force light waves into two separate rays, oscillating on two separate planes. Those rays would have different properties, properties that would cause them to bend in different degrees when passing through those crystals. And a crystal might be designed to deflect one—or both—of the rays. In the case of some crystals, only one ray might get through because the other is absorbed and turned into heat. In this manner, perhaps, Cyclops' mutant beams could be deflected and absorbed by the ruby quartz within his visor.

How is Cyclops able to see past the energy always flowing from his eyes? Whatever the nature of this energy, it is transparent to normal light. Although the energy emits a red glow, it must allow normal light to pass through it. Cyclops' may initially have perceived objects with a constant red tinge, but as experiments on normal humans have shown, the mind learns to compensate and adjust. In fact, you can perform this experiment yourself with sunglasses of different color tints. For instance, if you were to wear red glasses for a week or two, you would eventually stop noticing any tint at all. Once you removed the glasses, your adjusted/altered vision would perceive the world around you as green—the complementary color to red.

But, if his power beams are not a form of light or part of the electromagnetic spectrum, and all evidence suggests that they are not, then the most likely answer is that his optic beams are a form of exotic matter.

EXOTIC PARTICLES

Perhaps Cyclops's power is not energy but, in fact, matter—a stream of exotic particles, perhaps a particle beam of sorts. Another possibility is that his energy does not fit the criteria for any energy in this universe, it might originate in an alternate non-Einsteinian universe. In either case, the red pigmentation of the ray would be a side effect—just as heat is a side effect of normal energy processes.

That brings us back to those exotic particles mentioned earlier. Roughly speaking, most matter is composed of atoms, which are composed of subatomic particles called electrons, protons, and neutrons. But some matter is not built this way. Such matter is called "exotic," and has unusual properties, including its subatomic particles.

Exotic matter gets us into the area of higher physics, and it is in the area of exotic matter that we get a tantalizing glimpse at what might be the true source of Cyclops' power.

But first, let's examine how normal subatomic particles are constructed and then propose some alternatives. Most subatomic particles (protons, electrons and neutrons) are composed of quantum particles called quarks labeled: up, charm, top, down, strange, and bottom. These quantum particles, which you could call sub-subatomic particles, are glued together with "messenger particles," called gluons. These come in what physicists, in their whimsical way, call different "flavors": red, blue, and green.

We need to back up a little bit and return to the simple, old-fashioned subatomic level. At this level, the usual arrangement is, roughly speaking, electrons orbiting a nucleus composed of neutrons and protons. If you strip away the electron "shells," as they are sometimes called, then two possible types of matter can be formed. One is what is called the fourth state of matter: plasma. The first three states of matter are solid, liquid, and gas.

Plasma occurs with super-heated elements. The only naturally occurring plasmas on Earth are formed for a few fractions of a second in the path of a lightning bolt. The fiery flames of helium and hydrogen atoms burning in the sun are in a plasma state. Cooler plasma elements may exist between the stars in the cold of interstellar space. In fact, they might be part of the "dark matter" that theoretically makes up 90 percent of the universe. Because it is so common, plasma is not, strictly speaking, exotic matter.

But another form of electron-free matter is more exotic. It is what makes up a neutron star. Sometimes it is called neutronium. That is what remains when a star burns out and cools down. It is super-heavy, ultra-dense matter that theoretically collapses in on itself, and thereby becomes so heavy that it collapses through the continuum of our universe. This is called a black hole, and requires about three solar masses. A neutron star comprised solely of the mass of our sun would not form a black hole. But there are *highly* theoretical conditions under which micro-black holes might form.

It appears that on occasion Cyclops optic blast is composed of a small amount of neutronium particles. If he fired nothing but a concentrated stream of neutronium particles, they wouldn't tip over that 5,000-gallon tanker truck; they would punch a hole through it. But the idea of black holes punched through our universe leads us to other ideas, which we will come back to. First though, let's look at some more possibilities for exotic matter.

If we go down to the quantum level, we can imagine matter composed entirely of just one type of quantum instead of the usual brew of at least four types. Such hypothetical matter could have any sort of property, including properties that match those of Cyclops' beams. And if we go down past the quantum level, we can imagine matter composed of only one "color" of gluon, which also could have just about any property you can imagine. Such hypothetical exotic matter has never been found, and has probably not existed since the first few seconds after the Big Bang, so it is safe to ascribe unusual qualities to its behavior.

His eyes may be acting as a receiving and transmitting device due to the peculiar property of the exotic matter Cyclops is uniquely sensitive to. The only regret here is that long ago he had an accident, denying him the means to control it.

Some theoreticians believe that there might be many universes and not all of them have the same physical laws as ours. According to physicist and cosmologist Stephen Hawking, a few seconds after the Big Bang, several cosmic events happened just by accident. These accidents shaped the laws of our universe as basically defined by Aristotle with set theory; Newton and his three laws of Thermodynamics, Einstein with relativity, and Niels Bohr with quantum physics.

Our universe might be just one of an infinite number of bubble universes in the larger dimensionality of things. Every black hole that punches through the fabric of our universe might be opening into an alternate universe. And in some of those other universes, cause and effect might work quite differently.

HAVOK

Alex Summers, his older brother Scott and his parents, Christopher and Katherine Summers, were returning from a vacation when the plane they were traveling in was attacked by an alien, Shi'ar, spacecraft. As their damaged plane was going down in flames. Katherine pushed her sons out of the doomed craft with the only available parachute. Scott, who would later become Cyclops, the first X-Man, saved himself and his brother when his mutant power was triggered by the catastrophe. The Summers boys survived but sustained severe injuries requiring hospitalization. Orphaned, they were shortly thereafter separated.

Alex was placed in an orphanage in Omaha, Nebraska. Soon he was adopted and had little or no contact with his brother until many years later.

Like many orphans, Alex must have had severe control issues. Ever since the Shi'ar spacecraft attacked his family's plane (and there's something not many orphans share) his life, like the plane, seemed to spin out of control. Strangers now controlled his life. Still, Alex adapted to his new environment, excelling in school and developing an interest in both geology and archeology.

After Alex graduated from college, he rediscovered his mutant abilities. At the same time, a professor of archeology named Ahmet Abdol, also a mutant, became aware of a link between himself and Alex. Both of them apparently possessed the same latent mutant power to absorb and transform cosmic radiation. However, Abdol's ability to exercise his power was somehow "jammed" by Alex's physical presence. Abdol took Alex prisoner and brought him to his laboratory in Egypt. Once again, Alex found his life controlled by a stranger. That stranger, Professor Abdol, found a way to screen Alex's body from ambient cosmic radiation which, in turn, allowed Abdol to absorb the radiation himself, and utilize it to give himself special powers. But his plans for attaining further power were completely destroyed by the X-Men with Alex's help when his latent powers surfaced.

However, Alex now had another control problem: himself. He was unable to exercise any control over the energy his body radiated. This made him a considerable risk to others and so he decided to stay in the Egyptian desert rather than join the X-Men.

Of course his troubles didn't end there. Subsequently he was captured by a mutant-hunting robot Sentinel and brought to the headquarters of the Sentinels' controller. Once there, he was given the codename Havok and a costume with a chest display that monitored his buildup of cosmic energy. When the X-Men finally freed Alex, he decided to join the team.

Seeking to find a way to mentally control his power, he trained constantly and, using methods resembling biofeedback, eventually gained enough control to function as a team member.

ABSORPTION, STORAGE AND DISCHARGE OF COSMIC ENERGY

Havok constantly absorbs ambient "cosmic" energy into the cells of his body, transforms it, and releases it at will. The passage of this energy through air heats the air around it so intensely that the energy itself turns to plasma, the fourth state of matter. Havok usually directs these plasma waves along the length of his arms but he can also radiate them uniformly from his body. However, unlike his brother, Cyclops, Havok's energy blasts are not limited to one type of force or energy. Havok has the ability to project plasma, concussive force or a combination of both.

When Havok strikes out at an object with waves of intensely hot plasma, the abrupt and considerable rise in temperature can make objects shatter, explode, and even disintegrate. It might appear that a concussive force struck the objects but this is not, in fact, the case.

At its lowest, concussive, level, Havok's energy does not superheat the air. It simply projects waves of energy that have concussive impact.

When each of his body's power storage cells reaches its capacity, excess cosmic energy is immediately reemitted, but in negligible quantities. After the total expenditure of all of his available energy, it takes his body about five hours to recharge to its peak level.

Havok's directed power bursts require intense concentration on his part, and if he does this for extended periods of time, it exhausts him. If he just radiates his energy in all directions, it takes no concentration whatsoever, as that is how his power normally operates. On occasion he has needed a containment suit to keep his energy from continually discharging.

At full intensity, his power might be capable of leveling a mountain. While this has never been fully tested, an approximation of sorts was seen when he directed his powers at the Incredible Hulk, a walking green "mountain" in his own right.

Havok is immune to the intense heat he creates. He is also immune to Cyclops' power and vice versa.

GENETICS AND SIBLING SIMILARITIES

As we pointed out in Cyclops's entry, all forms of life radiate a form of energy—it's an inevitable side effect of metabolic processes. Almost all work in the material world of matter and electromagnetic energy produces heat as a side effect. Mammalian physiologies do more than just take advantage of this side effect—they deliberately generate heat to keep warm when it's cold outside. Many life forms also absorb energy. Plants absorb sunlight and use chlorophyll to turn it into metabolic energy. Humans and other species transform absorbed sunlight into Vitamin D.

In the case of Havok and certain other super-powered mutants, they are able to absorb and radiate energy on a scale that is vastly greater—perhaps in the area of 10^{10} times greater. (That's a somewhat arbitrary number based on the approximate difference between the frequencies of visible light and those of the higher forms of radiation. It's difficult, if not impossible, to compare the actual energy levels as the photon/quanta packets of light don't have a measurable one-for-one correspondence with the quantum particles of higher radiation. As all these particles lack any mass, you can't compare weight for weight, so it's difficult to know just how many photons are equivalent to how many quarks.)

COSMIC ENERGY

The science of physics does not recognize cosmic energy as such but it does acknowledge the existence of cosmic rays. These are highly charged particles that consist primarily of the nuclei of hydrogen, mostly protons. (The term "cosmic rays" is used loosely to refer to high-intensity radiation such as gamma rays, the sort of electromagnetic energy more usually emitted by nuclei. Technically, however, the term "cosmic rays" refers to high-energy particles.) This is, in a sense, the opposite of electricity, which is composed of negatively charged electrons. The origin of these cosmic rays is uncertain but one possibility is that they might come from supernovas.

These positively-charged protons have a range of energies from 10^8 to 10^{20} volts. This is enough energy to cause the super-heating necessary to create plasma. However, not many of these rays get through our atmosphere and the ones that do are usually under 10^{15} volts. Cosmic energy, then, must *not* be the same as cosmic rays. It must be an "unnatural" energy that doesn't follow our known physical laws.

PLASMA

Plasma, the fourth state of matter, comes after solids, liquids, and gasses. It is super-heated matter that consists of charged subatomic particles. When matter is heated to the degree that its the energy levels of its electron shells send them flying away, the result is a highly charged nucleus, much like a cosmic ray. It rarely occurs naturally on Earth but can be found briefly in the ionized trails of a lightning strike. Plasma is common in the high-energy environment of the sun, and radiates freely from our sun and stars.

It takes a long time for plasma to cool down, but when it does, the low-energy nuclei make up ultra-dense matter and that is the first step toward building a black hole. Eventually the plasma of the sun will cool and shrink. It takes the mass of about three suns to make a black hole, so our sun will never make it that far.

EINSTEIN'S BLUNDER?

Another possible source of Havok's powers is the energy that is always latent in the structure of the universe. When Einstein looked back on an early theory of his, the Cosmological Constant, an energy or weight that permeates space and counteracts gravity, he described it as his "greatest blunder." But now, some astronomers have reconsidered. Einstein's Cosmological Constant might make up 70 per cent of the universe.

The Cosmological Constant could be invoked to account for why the universe is not expanding as fast as expected. In the last 20 or 30 years, the notion of gravity due to invisible "dark matter" has been considered as an explanation for this extra force that holds the universe together. As yet, the practical implications of dark matter are unknown. What is known, however, is that energy can be extracted from pure vacuum. Noted physicist and author Dr. Robert L. Forward has designed a vacuum fluctuation battery based on the "Casimir Effect" which may or may not be related to the cosmological constant. It utilizes the Casimir Force, the short-range attraction between any two objects caused by the electromagnetic fluctuations always present in a vacuum. Dr. Forward's battery is a relatively simple device consisting of two plates of conductive material. The device is theoretical and has never been built. Its exact construction might entail a good deal of precise calculation, for the plates have to be at an exact distance from one another. Dr. Forward's device would probably produce a very small amount of energy. However, it does illustrate a physics phenomenon in which energy can be produced out of literally nothing, which is exactly what many of the X-Men seem capable to doing. Havok's rechanneling of "cosmic energy" might actually be a rechanneling of the Casimir Force.

PSIONIC POWER AND EXOTIC FORCES

Havok might actually have psionic abilities and use them to telekinetically master his powers. This would explain why it takes concentration and willpower for him to effect that control. However, psionic powers might also be a manifestation of the force itself, just as a light bulb's light is a manifestation of electricity. There might be a "bootstrapping" phenomenon at work here much like that which occurs when a computer boots-up and programs itself to program itself. In like manner, Havok could take an initial small amount of the exotic force, convert it to psionic power, and then use that to control greater amounts of the force. However, in this endeavor he must exercise supreme judgement: if he opens the floodgates too far—and hasn't budgeted enough psionic force to maintain control—he could be overwhelmed and have to bleed off the extra force until he can adjust the level of his psionic control.

UNUS THE UNTOUCHABLE

Before he died during a battle with the super hero Spider-Man, Angelo Unuscione had the power to project a force field that repelled any attack directed at him, which was why he was called "untouchable." Just as the Blob started out exploiting his talents as an attraction in the ring, so too did Unus. He was a pro wrestler until he embarked on what he hoped would be a more lucrative career as a criminal. He was one of the first villains to face the X-Men. His budding criminal career started off badly when the X-Men constructed a device that increased his power beyond his control: not only did he repel everything from him, including food and toiletries, he couldn't eat or bathe.

The X-Men, somewhat naively, neutralized the effects of their device in return for his promise to go straight. Unus soon returned to a life of crime. For a brief period he teamed up with Blob, Vanisher and Mastermind and later he was with Magneto's Brotherhood of Evil Mutants. It was in a battle with Spider-Man that his force field got beyond his control and repelled the air around him, causing him to die of suffocation.

POWERS

Unus was capable of generating around his body a wave-like field of invisible energy, probably psionic in nature, that deflected objects or energy beams.

While he controlled this with his mind, increasing the intensity of the field to deflect large objects, he could also harden this wave-like field into a solid barrier, an indestructible bubble around him. In this form, the field reached beneath his feet so that he actually stood and walked on the field, not on the floor or ground.

Normally he could turn the field on and off or raise or lower its intensity at will. He could even shut off a small portion of the field and allow himself to reach through the opening and touch his opponents while the rest of him remained untouchable.

Unus was the ultimate genetic solution to the basic biological challenge of how an organism could be kept sheltered from a hostile environment. In this respect his force field could be seen as an "outer skin." Like body armor, this field protected him from objects including bricks multiple high-speed projectiles, and from powerful energy blasts.

It's unlikely that Unus's force field was completely magnetic in nature: magnetic repulsion depends on opposite polarity, and most matter isn't polarized in the Einsteinian Universe. (See Exotic Electromagnetism, below.)

Gravity works in the opposite fashion, as do the remaining two forces of the universe, strong and weak nuclear force. So nothing in the Einsteinian universe will quite work.

Let's look outside.

WAVE-LIKE PSIONICS

That Unus's power appeared wave-like rather than simply as waves, implies a lot. Light, too, is wave-like. It is composed of photons, which are packets of quantum particles that are on the cusp of pure force, such as the positive and negative charges in protons and electrons and the material substance of the subatomic particles themselves.

Theoretically, psionic force is probably not made of photons but rather of some substance that is photon-like in that it is probably composed of packets of quantum-level particles halfway between energy and matter.

SELECTIVE FORCE FIELD

It was likely that the selective nature of his force field was not consciously controlled, but rather was a reflexive selectivity. Were he to make himself completely shielded from light, he would have become a perfect reflector and have a silvery appearance.

Certain aspects of Unus's power suggested that he utilized magnetic levitation force, especially when it came to his ability to repel gravity. Magnetic levitation, or "maglev" is used by certain high-speed trains. A maglev train has no wheels. It levitates above a track called a guideway and is propelled by magnetic fields.

When it is traveling, the train is suspended in the air above the tracks by magnetic repulsion and when it stops, it is docked by magnetic attraction. Alternating magnetic repulsion and attraction propels it. A series of powerful electromagnets located along the guide rail is used to create a moving magnetic wave. The maglev train is carried by this wave in the same manner as a surfer is carried by a wave in the ocean.

Unus might have been the equivalent of a living electromagnet if we view all matter as material to which Unus was selectively negatively polarized. Again, we're dealing with exotic forces and non-Einsteinian physics, but perhaps we ought to take at look at how an electromagnet works.

EXOTIC ELECTROMAGNETICISM

The concept of electromagnetism is pretty simple: when an electric current moves through a wire it produces a magnetic field. Although the field produced by a single wire isn't very powerful, if the wire is wound into a coil, the magnetic field will be intensified, especially if you place a piece of iron in the middle of the field.

A magnet can pick up a piece of steel or iron because its magnetic field flows into the metal and temporarily turns it into a magnet, and these two magnets are attracted to one another. This happens because there are small magnetic regions inside the metal called domains. Normally they are arranged helter-skelter and their poles cancel each other out. But the effect of magnetic force upon the iron aligns the domains' poles. This creates a temporary magnet.

The strength of a magnet depends upon its size and the amount of the current running through it. Scrapped cars are piled into heaps by giant electromagnets in junkyards. On the opposite side of the scale, tiny electromagnets can be used medically for extracting splinters—provided that the splinters are metal.

Of course, if Unus had indeed functioned as a living electromagnet he must have had tremendous selective control over what he would and would not repel. And this could be one reason why when that control failed, it had such extreme consequences.

SUPERCONDUCTIVITY

Unus's powers could also be seen as taking the concept of superconductivity an "eXtra" step beyond its current uses. Superconductors are materials that under certain conditions provide no resistance and therefore conduct electricity without any loss.

Dr. Palmer N. Peters, a physicist at the National Aeronautics and Space Administration's Space Science Laboratory in Huntsville, Alabama, experimented with a small ceramic disk that was cooled to the point that it acted as a superconductor. Dr. Peters held a magnet close to the disk, which was in a dish filled with liquid nitrogen. To his amazement, when he pulled the magnet away from the disk, the disk seemed to disappear. He finally discovered it dangling below the magnet, seemingly in midair, caught in the magnetic field. As the disk warmed up, it lost its superconductive quality and escaped from the magnet.

This episode illustrated the possibility that scientists, and possibly doctors, could manipulate objects that were in enclosed environments—even the human body—via this suspension phenomenon.

Scientists believe that the suspension effect occurs when a superconductor's field is coupled to a magnet's field in a manner that causes the superconductor to act with a kind of "electromagnetic sentience."

If superconductivity could be achieved at, say, room

temperature, its applications would be many. In view of that, scientists are experimenting with different materials and making rapid progress in raising the temperature at which superconductivity occurs.

How could this apply to Unus? If, by virtue of the exotic nature of his power—and possibly, his body—he could have functioned as a superconductor at "room temperature," then perhaps his repelling power was really the result of his dispelling any resistance between his exotic "magnetism" and the object upon which he was focused. Perhaps he was not only a living "magnet" but a living "superconductor" of exotic forces resembling magnetism but affecting all matter.

As we've said, it was unlikely that the selective nature of Unus's force field was consciously controlled. If Unus were to have had such fine control over his shielding from gravity, he would be able to levitate, even to fly, and he would not have suffered the asphyxiating fate that he did. In effect, it could be said that Unus was a mutant whose mutation was a blessing and a curse, for it carried a genetic weak link that ultimately proved fatal.

SHADOWCAT

Born and raised in Deerfield, Illinois, Kitty was another mutant whose power didn't manifest itself until puberty. At the age of 13, she began to have severe headaches. These migraines proved to be symptoms of her the awakening of her mutant power, the ability to pass through solid objects which she calls "phasing."

After locating Kitty with Cerebro, his mutant-finding device, Professor X accompanied the X-Men Storm, Colossus, and Wolverine to find and enroll her in his School for Gifted Youngsters. Despite a similar and simultaneous recruitment attempt by his rival Emma Frost, at the time the headmistress of the Massachusetts Academy (a school that also recruited mutants, but for more sinister purposes), Kitty opted for Professor Xavier's school.

Kitty proved to be a brilliant student and proficient in both academics and the rigorous combat skills required of the X-Men. Strong willed, she rebelled at Professor X's initial code name designation of her, Sprite. For a time she used the *nom de guerre* Ariel before finally settling on Shadowcat.

PHASING

Shadowcat calls her remarkable mutant power "phasing." While phasing, she can pass through solid matter and any sort of physical projectiles or energy rays will pass right through her. However, psionic or mystical powers can affect her while in this immaterial state.

Not only can she become immaterial, she can also "merge" with another person or object, thereby allowing them to "phase" as well. The first obvious benefit is the fact that when she phases, her clothing doesn't collapse in a heap on the floor, but remains on her body. Additionally, it has come in handy when, for instance, during a battle she has to bring another member of the X-Men team along with her through a solid barrier.

In most cases, she can phase through anything, even people, without any ill effects either to herself or the object she's passing through. The most notable exception is when she phases through an object possessing any sort of electrical system, her presence disrupts the operation of that system.

Her one limitation while phasing is that she has to maintain constant mental control over her atoms. If she doesn't, the expanded (i.e. loosened) bondage of her atoms could completely dissolve and she would disappear.

VIBRATION AND STRING THEORY

So, how does she go through Wall B in order to get from Point A to Point C? Science gives us two possible answers.

One of the ways that Shadowcat could pass through objects is by controlling the vibration of the molecules that comprise her matter. Modern theoretical physics offers a possibility with its "string theories." String theories are the grandchildren of Einstein's first tries at putting together a unified field. They are highly theoretical, unproved, and maybe even unprovable. These theories use at least 12 dimensions, but some use up to 26 dimensions.

Looking at the universe of energy and matter through the prism of string theory, we discover that everything vibrates. If Shadowcat can charge her body with the high levels of energy needed to alter the vibration level of the portions of cosmic string that make up her matter, she could elevate herself to a high level of energy that would pass through matter. In effect, she would become free energy.

Consider it this way: Light is near the top of the electromagnetic scale, and is made of packets of photons which are halfway between concrete subatomic particles and the more abstract concept of a wave. (In fact, they're called "wavicles," half wave, half particle.) And this is the range where we see the high-energy quantum particles that can fly through matter.

Lower down the scale, we have electricity. Compared to light, electricity is reasonably concrete. Although we consider it to be energy, it's composed of electrons, just like one third of all regular matter.

Much further down the scale is matter.

If Shadowcat is converting herself into energy, a great deal depends upon the degree of matter dissolution that takes place during the transition. Energy released by the dissolution of matter into its component particles is a long-winded way of saying it explodes. When it happens on an atomic level you have a nuclear explosion. Since we don't have explosions when Shadowcat phases or returns to solid form (because reverting back would require just as much energy as was released when she converted to energy), if this is the way she phases, she's obviously avoided this problem.

SPINTRONICS

There's another possible explanation for how Shadowcat can phase. Obviously, to actually make two objects pass through each other safely would require coordination of billions of particles. Believe it or not, technology already exists that actually does this. It's called Spintronics. Although it's not "phasing," it behaves very similarly, but so far only works with electrons. Perhaps someday it will be applied to other particles as well.

Electrostatic repulsion is the force that keeps subatomic objects from passing through one another. The electrons repel each other, like when you have two like-charged magnetic poles close together. But instead of having a positive or negative charge, the electrons have what is called "spin." Spin is determined to be "up" or "down."

Normally the spin of electrons is a random mix of up and down. If these states could be ordered, much like in the way that magnetism or light can be polarized, maybe the states of both objects could be coordinated so that one could pass through the other.

This principle is called "Spintronics," "Giant Magneto-Resistance" (GMR), or "Tunneling Magnetic Junction" (TMJ). It is used in new computer memory chips that should be commercially available within a few years. Tiny magnetic fields are used to control the spin of electrons and this new sort of spin control is used in conjunction with another quantum effect known as "tunneling." Tunneling is where current moves from one conductive layer to another in electronic chips with layers of conductive materials. When it does this, the current switches its spin. When these electrons switch their spins, they pass through each other—in effect "phasing" just as Shadowcat does.

The spin control and electron tunneling that we can effect at the level of micro-electronics in the laboratory with tiny magnetic fields, Shadowcat might be able to perform with many more tiny fields to control both the spin of not just electrons, but all the fundamental particles in her own body (and the bodies or objects that she's holding), and the spin of whatever she passes through.

She could polarize the matter she's going through, and herself. Or she could change the polarity of her particles, one by one, and match them against the matter she has to pass through, particle by particle, so that the repulsive force that makes matter hard would become an attractive force that pulls her through. At atomic distances the strong nuclear force takes over. The repulsive force wouldn't be a problem anymore and, with all that empty space between particles at that level, her particles wouldn't get close enough to become ensnared by the strong force, so she could slide through without getting stuck.

She might not even have to reverse the polarity of all her particles. Maybe she only needs to control the spin on a sizeable percentage of them, depending on the density the matter she must phase through. By reverse polarization of the spin of portions of air, she could climb imaginary steps as if they were as concrete as, well, concrete.

It's no wonder that she disrupts electronics when she passes through them. She could be polarizing the spin of all the current in the device, and drastically changing the resistance and conductance factors of the circuits. Stray current must be tunneling like crazy from one circuit to the next.

To polarize her particles, she must have the same psionic mechanisms for micro-control of the quantum mechanical world as other the other X-Men. Her vulnerability to psionic power is not surprising if psionics are composed of some of the exotic energies we've postulated. She could use small magnetic fields to coordinate the spin of particles. Psionics might not have anything to do with particles but she could use some of the same control mechanisms as the psionic mutants, which are, basically, quantum level effects.

Shadowcat's control over her talent has grown with practice. She rarely weakens from exertion of her talent anymore. That's good, because as she's discovered as she gets older life gets more complicated, and in the X-Men's case, more dangerous.

NIGHTCRAWLER

Kurt Wagner led a life unusual even by X-Men standards. Abandoned under mysterious circumstances, he was found by the gypsy queen and sorceress Margali Szardos who took him to her gypsy circus where he was raised by the group. Years later, Kurt, whose powers had by then matured, left the circus after it was purchased by an American businessman and taken to Florida. Returning to Germany, Kurt was attacked by superstitious villagers who believed he was a demon responsible for the recent deaths of several children. Fortunately for him, Professor X was nearby, in the process of searching for new recruits for the X-Men. He found Kurt just in time to rescue him. He joined the X-Men, adopting as his code name, Nightcrawler.

POWERS

Unlike almost all other mutants with super powers, Nightcrawler was born with major physical differences—pointed ears and teeth, only two fingers and a thumb on each hand, only two toes and an amazingly flexible projection on the heel of each foot. What's more, his eyes are yellow and have no pupil—although this doesn't prevent him from having near-perfect night vision. His entire body appears to be covered in coarse short blue fur which may actually be mutated human hair (see segment on testosterone in the Wolverine entry).

His spine is more flexible than an ordinary human being's, which allows him to spend much of his time in a crouching posture without giving him a backache. More importantly, to his career as an X-Man, it also enables him to perform contortionist-like feats. Nightcrawler also has a pointed, prehensile tail. This tail can not only grasp items but also perform complex tasks such as fencing with a sword. It has also proven strong enough to support his weight and, occasionally, the weight of another person as well.

But his greatest ability is that of teleportation.

TELEPORTATION

Nightcrawler teleports by displacing himself into the under-documented "Darkforce" dimension, which he travels through until he reemerges in our time-space continuum at his desired location. The entire process occurs so quickly—nearly instantaneously—that he is unaware of having visited another dimension at all. His teleportation power is not psionic but, rather, the result of a chemical biophysical reaction that he triggers mentally.

One side effect of Nightcrawler's teleportation is the burst of smoke and a stench reminiscent of burning brimstone. This is a chemical reaction by-product of teleportation. Nightcrawler's teleportation is invariably accompanied by the muffled sound of an implosion of air rushing to fill the vacuum caused by his body's dimensional shift.

Nightcrawler has very limited extrasensory power that prevents him from teleporting himself into a solid wall. The farther he teleports, the more difficult and tiring it is. He most likely has some automatic mechanism that compensates for his momentum, enabling him to "land" safely. Again, it's an automatic compensatory action performed without any conscious effort on his part.

Nightcrawler's teleportation ability depends on his ability to visualize his destination—either by being able to see it or from having seen it in the past. He can teleport himself, the clothes he wears, and within limits, a certain amount of additional matter that is in contact with him. He can even carry a buddy along with him.

The trip itself can be quite unsettling as any matter traveling through the Darkforce dimension is slightly displaced. By taking a foe through a rapid succession of teleports, he can easily stun them into insensibility.

It is easier for him to teleport between north and south along Earth's magnetic lines of force than is it for him to east and west, against them. Under the best circumstances, teleporting only himself and his costume, he can send himself about two miles east-to-west and up to three miles north-to-south. It is difficult and dangerous for him to teleport upward. He once made a vertical teleportational jump of two miles but had to push himself to his physical limits.

When he transports a passenger over even moderate distances, they both feel weakened and ill to the point of exhaustion. Teleportation over further distances might lead to death.

His momentum is retained throughout the teleportation

process so that he arrives at exactly the same momentum with which he left. If he were to fall from a great height, he could not teleport himself towards the ground in an effort to slow his descent and save himself. Even if he teleported, he would land at the same velocity with which he was falling.

The big problem with teleportation is that the world turns. Yes, this is probably not news to you, but the Earth spins extremely fast. So we are all in constant motion.

Even though Nightcrawler seldom teleports more than three miles, when he does that to the north or south, it would amount to a velocity change of about 44 feet per second, for the Earth spins much faster at the equator than it does north or south of it.

The diameter of the Earth at the equator is 7,926 miles. It makes a complete rotation in 24 hours (one day). The diameter at the exact center of the north and south poles is zero. The poles spin at zero miles per hour. The equator spins at about 1037.5 miles per hour, or .2882 miles per second.

The world is also revolving around the Sun, so we are in motion from that. And the solar system is spiraling around the huge black hole at the center of our galaxy, the Milky Way, so we move with that, too. And the entire danged galaxy is flying away from the center of the universe, still in motion from the Big Bang.

All told, we all have a lot of momentum. So if you abruptly pick us up and plunk us down in the middle of somewhere else that isn't traveling at *exactly* the same speed as we are, in *exactly* the same direction, *zip*, off we go, flying into the nearest wall like a bug against a windshield.

Force equals mass times acceleration, and we all have a

lot of force—and acceleration—inherent in our lives. If that force is misdirected, the results can be disastrous, as, for example, when we're sitting comfortably in a car traveling at 60 miles per hour, unaware, really, of how fast we're moving and how much force we contain... until someone suddenly hits the brakes.

Nightcrawler has to have an automatic mechanism that compensates for momentum. This automatic compensatory action is controlled subconsciously and is most likely performed by his rear brain.

GRAVITY: A MATTER OF SPACE-TIME

Before we examine how Nightcrawler teleports through space, let's check out exactly what space is. Space is not simply nothing. Space is dimensionality, specifically three dimensions if you're considering our space-time continuum. And space is also related to matter in that, if you have a great deal of matter in one place—like a black hole—space collapses and everything "rolls downhill" into the collapsed space.

Another word for this is gravity.

If you consider the planet Earth to be a depression in the fabric of space, it has enough mass to not only bend the fabric of space but to create a lot of gravity as well. Our planet has an equatorial diameter of almost 8,000 miles and most of that is rock and metal. That's enough mass so that it literally bends the fabric of space and creates a lot of gravity.

Any one or thing attempting to escape that gravitational pull must have sufficient momentum and/or the ability to "step" outside regular space. In fact, that's one way to take a shortcut through space: just bend it with a lot of mass. Unfortunately, that amount of mass would pull you in with it. However, since Nightcrawler can control his momentum, he might also have control over mass and gravity, just as Juggernaut and Blob seem to.

If he doesn't follow the natural curve of three-dimensional space, he must be able to go outside of it. The current thinking, as we've mentioned before, is that our universe is composed of about 12 dimensions. However, all but four are rolled up into unimaginable thinness. We can only guess that a dimensional traveler is able to compress himself in a similar manner, without any bodily harm. That would mean that in addition to his control over momentum and mass, Nightcrawler has yet another power.

TIMESHARING

In addition to his control over space, momentum, and mass, Nightcrawler also has limited control over time as well. It is a cliché of fantastic fiction to refer to time as the fourth dimension. This is not strictly true. We have no effective way of describing the other dimensions of our universe other than the language of mathematics. However, we can say that if you could step far enough outside our three dimensions you would be able to see all four walls of a room and the floor... *and* the ceiling at once. You would also be able to see that room from its construction to its ultimate demolition. The universe would appear as a bubble that was blown and collapsed all at once, somewhat like a time-lapse exposure. Time is not the fourth dimension, but it would, theoretically, be visible in its entirety from an extra-dimensional vantage point. From that vantage, one might be able to enter our 3-D sub-space at any point in time.

Were one to have some control over time, it would be

possible to alter one's momentum, for force equals mass times acceleration, remember? And acceleration is movement over time. Were one's movement taking place over a shorter period of time, one would have less velocity . . . and less momentum.

MULTIPLEXING

Acceleration is movement over time. If, prior to teleportation, Nightcrawler were to hopscotch through time, so that he actually appeared here for every other 60th of a second—perhaps the shortest interval in which the human eye can register an image—he would appear to be here but would in fact be "multiplexing" in much the same manner that different communication signals are sent in the same satellite transmission.

For example, long distance telephone calls sound continuous to both caller and receiver, but some are actually being multiplexed. This means that every other fraction of a second of the transmitted signal is missing, although no actual sound is lost. In effect, it's a process of slicing and dicing time to move more signal through it.

Time Division Multiplexing, implemented in the 1980s, chops a data stream into "time" slices and interleaves them with other data streams. Nothing goes missing or is eliminated: It's just that more happens—in this case, is transmitted—through the spaces in between.

If Nightcrawler is actually hopscotching through time in order to gain momentum, he is automatically compensating for speed buildup and reduction as he enters and exits the Darkforce continuum. What's more, as he slices and dices time he can slip back and forth between the dimensions, seeming to travel instantaneously.

For example, when non-mutant humans walk, we utilize all sorts of actions to maintain balance, momentum, and direction. Otherwise, we'd spend a great deal more time on the ground, picking ourselves up. So, too, might Nightcrawler spend a great deal more time in the Darkforce universe—which obviously doesn't smell as nice as ours does—if he couldn't automatically control and hasten his entrances and departures.

UNIQUE AMONG PEERS

The final analysis of Nightcrawler is that in a group noted by its extraordinary abilities, he is unique. The odds against an organism with his physiology surviving past birth are astronomical. Nightcrawler's successful existence is proof that the X-genes also contain the genetic information to sustain lifeform shapes that are dramatically different from the human form.

NIGHTCRAWLER'S MOMENTUM: THE MATH EQUATION

Would Nightcrawler's teleportation of a few miles north or south cause a large change in his speed (due to the earth's rotation)? We thought we'd do the math on one example to find out.

The change in speed would be largest if one started at the North Pole (linear speed zero) three miles due south. He would then be rotating along with the Earth on a circle of radius R*sin(3/R) where R=3963 is the Earth's radius. This comes out to be about three miles, so the circumference of the circle he moves on is 2*Pi*3 miles or about 18.5 miles. So after teleporting he's moving 18.5 miles in 24 hours, giving a velocity of 18.5/24 mph or about 0.785 mph. So his change in speed is only 0.785 mph (about 1.15 feet per second).

What is the speed of a point on the surface of the earth due to the earth's rotation? Consider the speed of a body rotating on a circle of radius R is R*w where w is the angular speed of rotation (expressed in radians). For an object that rotates once every 24 hours like the earth, the angular speed is 2*Pi/24 radians per hour. So the speed of a body at the equator is 3963*2Pi/24 miles per hour (since the radius R of the earth is 3963 and w is 2*Pi/24), or about 1037.5 miles per hour. To convert to miles per second, divide by 60*60 to get about .2882 miles per second.

What change in Nightcrawler's speed would he get from teleporting three miles north or south? What is the change in speed due to the earth's rotation that results from teleporting three miles north or south?. The change in speed depends on what latitude you start with. Let a represent the angle above the equator that you are at. The change in speed due to teleporting three miles north at an angle a above the equator is APPROXIMATELY (Pi/4)*sin(a) miles per hour.

Starting at the North Pole, a is Pi/2 radians, sin(a) is 1, so the change in speed is about Pi/4 mph or about .7854 mph or about 1.15 feet per second.

Starting at the equator, a is 0 radians, sin(a) is 0, and the approximation above says the change in speed is zero. Of course this is just an approximation. One can compute the actual change in speed to be about .0002973 miles per hour. (The actual change in speed for a 3-mile north-south teleport is given by (2*Pi/24)*R*(cos(a+3/R)−cos(a)) miles per hour, R=3963 miles)

Starting somewhere between the equator and the North

Pole, the change in speed due to teleporting three miles north or south will be somewhere between these two extremes. So the change in velocity will be negligible, less than stepping off a moving sidewalk at the airport.

PHYSICAL ATTRIBUTES

The X-Men who stick out most in a crowd are those who have physical mutations. Angel has wings, Wolverine has claws, and Beast is, well, a beast. (Nightcrawler's physiology is secondary to his teleporting ability, thus he's in the Exotic Powers section.)

As different as some of the X-Men appear, they are still human, even if some of them call themselves "Homo superior." Their DNA is almost identical. It would take only a rearrangement of a small percentage of human DNA to produce enormous changes in physical appearance, even the drastically different appearance of Colossus.

Like Colossus, Iceman and Rogue can change their appearance but the latter two can change more than just themselves. They might have some access to the same exotic forces as such powerful X-Men as Cyclops and Havok. This might mean that their appearances are due to an entirely different set of factors. Or it might mean that the mutations of other X-Men are reversible in some sense. Certainly we have seen the appearance of Beast change. Once again, we are reminded of the moral: don't judge people by their appearance.

WOLVERINE

The X-Man known in private life as Logan is the most mysterious, volatile, independent and dangerous of the X-Men. He is the best at what he does, and what he does is hunt and kill. His attitude about combat has often placed him in direct conflict with Professor X and other members of the X-Men team. At the same time, there has proved to be no one more loyal than Logan, who has demonstrated innumerable times his willingness to risk his own life for his friends. (Of course, part of that willingness is the knowledge that it's virtually impossible to kill him.) No one knows his true age or his full name. In fact, even his memories of his early life are fragmented and suspect. One thing that is certain is that his adamantium skeleton and claws were bonded to him in a lengthy and painful procedure conducted in the mysterious Weapon X program. For a long time, it was thought that claws were also grafted onto his nerves and the bones of his forearms, but it later seemed that these were actually fantastically strong organic outgrowths, part of his mutant nature.

CELLULAR REGENERATION

Wolverine heals much faster than normal folks do. He can regenerate large damaged or even destroyed areas of tissue and bone. Of course, the more severe the injury, the longer it takes to heal. For example, a sword wound that went entirely through his torso took nearly two months to heal.

Many of his senses are comparable to those of certain animals. He has a sense of smell as sensitive as that of a tracking animal such as a dog or wolf. His acute senses are due in part to his power of cellular regeneration. The cells of his sense organs do not atrophy over time as they would in an ordinary human. It is not yet known whether Wolverine could regenerate an entire organ or body part.

The limits of Wolverine's regenerative ability have not been fully tested. Doing so under laboratory conditions would require an extraordinary breach of ethical conduct (the Weapon X program notwithstanding). As for testing under combat conditions, well, given what it would take to get to such an extreme situation, one can only hope that he's never in a fight that literally tears him limb from limb.

Cell growth is dependent on protein synthesis, which is, in turn, dependent on ribosome synthesis. Ribosomes are particles rich in ribonucleic acid (RNA) which participate in the synthesis of proteins within cells. RNA plays a key role in cell metabolism, specifically during the stages of division and protoplasmic growth so important to healing damaged tissue.

A wide variety of hormones play a major role in the stimulation of cell growth which is what causes healing. Steroids are one group that stimulate a certain type of cell growth—muscle cells in particular, and we can assume that

Wolverine must have hyped-up steroidal activity, stimulated by damage to his bodily tissues.

Enzymes are complex catalysts of biological origin, protein in nature and found in all cells and the blood, which function to increase the speed of a reaction without being used in the reaction itself. We must assume that Wolverine's body is packed with exotic enzymes which contribute to his remarkable healing powers.

Wolverine's fast-healing factor would have to call upon a cocktail mix of hormones, enzymes, and other growth factors. As anyone who has to take a variety of prescription drugs knows, the mixing of different drugs can have unexpected, sometimes fatal side-effects. Hormonal interactions and imbalances can create a wide range of behaviors. If his hormonal functions are generally overstimulated that might account for his berserker rages. Here are just a few of the hormones involved in growth and healing that might figure prominently in Wolverine's amazing healing patterns:

Platelet-Derived Growth Factor: a growth hormone carried in the blood platelets. It is released when platelets adhere to traumatized tissues. Connective tissue cells near the traumatized region respond by initiating the process of replication and healing.

Sermorelin: a trigger for releasing the human growth hormone somatotropin, which is often used to stimulate growth in children with a growth hormone deficiency.

Gonadorelin: a hormone released by the hypothalamus that stimulates the secretion of follicle-stimulating hormone (FSH) and luteinizing hormone (LH) from the pituitary gland, both of which contribute to cell growth and development.

HORMONES AND GROWTH

The main hormones concerned with growth are pituitary growth hormone, thyroid hormone, the sex hormones testosterone and estrogen, and the pituitary gonadotropic (sex-gland-stimulating) hormones. Since new cell growth is a primary part of the healing process, these hormones must all be involved in Wolverine's cellular functions.

PITUITARY AND SEX HORMONES

The pituitary gland is a small oval endocrine gland that lies at the base of the brain. It's often called the master gland because all other endocrine glands rely upon its secretions for stimulation.

The pituitary has two distinct lobes, anterior and posterior. The anterior lobe secretes at least six hormones: growth hormone, which stimulates overall body growth, ACTH (adrenocorticotropic hormone) which controls steroid hormone secretion in the adrenal cortex and throtropic hormone, which stimulates the activity of the thyroid gland and the gonadotropic which, as the name indicates, controls growth and reproductive activity of the gonads.

The posterior lobe secretes antidiuretic hormone, which causes water retention by the kidneys, and oxytocin, necessary for uterine contractions and the release of milk by the mammary glands.

Pituitary growth hormone, a protein with known amino acid composition, is secreted by the pituitary gland throughout life. Exactly what its function is in the adult is not clear, but in the child it is necessary for growth; without it dwarfism results.

There is a "call and response" interaction exists between

the pituitary gland and the gonads which results in sexual maturation in both male and female humans.

In the males, the testes secrete steroids called androgens, which are responsible for the maintenance of male characteristics and behavior. FSH (follicle-stimulating hormone) from the pituitary gland stimulates the growth of the testes and promotes within them the cell divisions that result in the production of mature sperm.

LH (luteinizing hormone), often called ICSH, or interstitial-cell-stimulating hormone in males, from the pituitary gland promotes the development of the testes, which, in turn, secretes the steroid hormone testosterone, which is the most important vertebrate androgen.

Testosterone is necessary for the development of the external genitals in the male fetus and, at puberty, its increased levels are responsible for male secondary sex characteristics such as facial hair.

Testosterone has been credited with affecting not only the production of body hair but aggressive behavior in human males. We might argue that Wolverine, Nightcrawler and Beast have high levels of testosterone shown in their aggressive behavior and unusual "hairstyles."

Only small amounts of testosterone circulate between birth and puberty, but at puberty, in response to pituitary luteinizing hormones, testosterone is secreted in large amounts, triggering most of the changes of male puberty, especially the adolescent growth spurt.

The female sex hormones, collectively called estrogens, are first secreted in quantity at puberty by cells in the ovary. They cause growth of the internal reproductive organs and development of secondary sexual characteristics. The adolescent growth spurt in the female is probably caused by testosterone-like substances (androgens) secreted by the adrenal gland in both male and female.

ADRENAL GLANDS

Wolverine obviously relies a great deal upon adrenalin and the source of that is located in the adrenal glands on the upper inner surface of his kidneys. The adrenal glands produce epinephrine (adrenalin) and, to a much lesser extent, norepinephrine as well as other chemicals such as chromogranins, enkephalins, and neuropeptide Y—hormones that are released into the bloodstream. Epinephrine, in particular, affects many different types of tissues throughout the body, and prevents hypoglycemia (low blood sugar) by inhibiting the release of insulin, resulting in a greater amount of glucose available to the brain.

Although Wolverine may in fact have an oversupply of adrenaline at his disposal, he doesn't seem to suffer from hypercorticism, specifically Cushing's syndrome, named for neurosurgery pioneer Harvey Cushing. It's an illness resulting from overactivity of the adrenal cortex and often results in progressive weakness and muscle wasting among its sufferers.

THYROID GLANDS

One of the primary regulators of human metabolism is the thyroid metabolism is the thyroid gland, located in the neck, which produces thyroid hormones. Thyroid hormones, while necessary for normal growth, do not themselves stimulate growth (and healing). Rather, they function as triggers to stimulate the release of growth-activating hormones.

When the thyroid gland malfunctions, hyperthyroidism (or thyrotoxicosis) can occur. This causes the metabolism's activity to increase, and can result in excessive hunger combined with weight loss. Increased nervousness and emotional instability are other symptoms. The most common cause of hyperthyroidism is Graves' disease, named for the Irish physician Robert J. Graves.

Although, again, Wolverine just might have a hyperactive metabolism, it's probably not due to Graves' disease, which involves the body's immune system and often generates autoantibodies, harmful to the body's own tissues. Given Wolverine's amazing powers of healing, it's doubtful that he suffers from hyperthyroidism.

HORMONAL IMBALANCE

However, some of Wolverine's odd physical abilities could possibly be the result of hormonal imbalances. Consider, for example, the effect of too much estrogen on a human male: a distinct feminization of the features will usually occur, including the development of breasts and a high-pitched voice. The reverse effects, hirsutism and muscle development, result when a human female receives too much testosterone. Most of us are familiar with the mood swings associated with both Pre-Menstrual Syndrome (PMS) and Post-Partum Depression, when hormonal imbalances can create both physical and emotional problems for the sufferers.

Perhaps one of the results of odd hormonal distribution in Wolverine's physiological system is the development of his extraordinarily acute senses.

ACUTE SENSORY RECEPTORS

Wolverine's amazing senses are comparable in sensitivity and acuteness to those of certain animals. Certainly he exhibits a sense of smell as sensitive as that of a tracking animal, i.e. a dog or wolf. He can see in near-total darkness and hear whispers from quite a distance. His senses of taste and touch are equally powerful.

In normal humans, the receptor neurons in each of our sensory systems deal with different kinds of energy: mechanical, electromagnetic, or chemical. All these receptor neurons turn a stimulus into an electrochemical nerve impulse, which is what the brain uses to operate.

One reason that Wolverine's senses would be greater than ours is the possibility that he actually has more sensory receptors—developed under the influence of hormones and other growth factors.

To understand how powerfully enhanced Wolverine's senses and abilities are, it may help to compare and contrast them with the workings of the basic five senses of average Homo Sapiens.

Although there are many senses, more than have been consistently classified, the commonly recognized senses are detected by only five types of sensory receptors.

Type of Receptor	Type of Response Stimuli
Photoreceptors	Light
Chemoreceptors	Smell, taste, and internal sensing in digestive and circulatory systems

VISION

Vision is the most immediate and accessible of our senses. The visual system uses about 25% of the cerebral cortex. The retina is a sheet of receptors at the back of the eye and is the only part of the brain that is visible from outside the skull. Any doctor can easily see the retina with just a peek through the opthalmoscope. There are two types of photoreceptor cells in the retina. These are rods and cones. They seem to have evolved from hair cells.

Rods detect light levels, which means they only pick up black and white images. Most animals have only rods in their retinas. For humans, rods are more common in a circular zone near the edge of the eye. This has a few interesting implications, which we'll get to in just a bit. Wolverine's enhanced vision might be due to a different distribution of rods and cones. However, there is only so much space for these in the retina so if you increase the count of one, you have to decrease the count of another. Essentially, you must trade color perception for the more detailed perception of black and white, which is largely what enables us to perceive motion.

Perhaps Wolverine actually has *less* color perception and more therefore heightened motion perception. The rods that perceive motion and black and white images are so light sensitive that we can see at night with only starlight to guide us. Of course we can't read a newspaper by starlight but we can usually avoid walking into a tree.

Rhodopsin is the light-sensitive receptor protein in the disk membranes of rod cells. It reacts to the tiniest bits of light. As mentioned in the Scarlet Witch entry, the rods in our eyes are actually so sensitive that they can react to a single photon. That's pretty impressive when you consider that a photon is a packet of quantum particles. It's not only smaller than an atom; it's smaller than an electron! This means that we can directly perceive events on a quantum scale.

It would be difficult to increase the sensitivity of a rod. One could only increase the amount of rods. Some animals with enhanced night vision, such as owls, have larger retinas. Conceivably, Wolverine could also share this attribute.

Rods are unevenly distributed across the retina. There are ten times more rods than cones, except in the fovea—the center of the retina—which is the cones' turf. They are highly concentrated in the fovea to about a square millimeter. Consequently, the fovea is less sensitive to light than the rest of the retina. To detect a faint star at night, try turning your head slightly to the side so that the star's light hits more of the sensitive rods in your eyes. Our peripheral vision—images we perceive at the side of our retina—also detects motion better than the center of the eye. This makes good sense in terms of evolutionary survival. We see motion at the edges of our vision well enough to prevent somebody from sneaking up on us.

Cones, the other photoreceptor cells, detect colors, and are clustered in the center of the retina, or fovea. There are three kinds of cones, for the three primary colors, red, yellow and blue, which divide the visible frequency of the light spectrum into three equal portions. We perceive color as a combination of these hues.

Opsins are chemicals that bind to cone cells and make those cells sensitive to light of a particular wavelength, or color. Humans have three different forms of opsin chemicals coded for each of the three primary colors. There are also three genes on the X chromosome, one for each color.

THE OPSIN CHEMICALS

When light strikes the rod and cone receptors, it makes the chemical rhodopsin for the rods, and three other opsin chemicals for the cones, break down. This creates what the researchers call "membrane potential" that becomes "action potential". The point is that the signal gets sent to neurons that connect to the optic nerve.

The optic nerve connects to the occipital lobe of the brain. It takes a fraction of a second to replenish the opsin chemicals, more with a stronger light, and in their absence, we see a negative after-image. Try turning on a really bright 1,000 watt bulb in a completely dark room and then quickly turn it off. You will see an extremely detailed negative image for up to a few seconds. Turn around and turn the light on and you will be completely disoriented.

Our color vision extends from the low frequencies verging into infrared, which can be generated by simple heat, to the high range of ultraviolet. We can see in the 400–700 nanometer (nm) range, a small portion of the electromagnetic spectrum, the visible light spectrum. At the high end, light with wavelengths less than 400 nm is ultraviolet light. At the low end, light with wavelengths longer than 700 nm is infrared light.

As with all things in the biological world, there's a good deal of variability in the range of color that people can perceive. Most of us have some minor degree of color blindness. A few are completely color blind. And at the opposite end of the scale, some are able to see farther into the infrared and ultraviolet because their cones are more sensitive and their chemical reactions are more easily triggered. There is anecdotal evidence of people whose cones even react to X-rays.

RESOLUTION AND DISTANCE

Some people have been able to spot seagoing ships on the horizon, about 90 miles away. We can see things as small as the point of a pin and the pores in our skin. We have the best resolution at the center, or fovea, or our vision. After that, curiously, we tend to see better at the bottom of our vision than at the top. This development might have evolutionary roots. Our prehistoric ancestors were hunter-gatherers. The ones with the best "bottom vision" would be the ones to first spot food and/or danger on the ground. Those with the best sight (along with other desirable abilities) would be the ones who survived long enough to pass that trait to the next generation.

HEARING: SOUND CONVERSION TO NERVE IMPULSES

Hearing detects sound waves in the air, water, or any other conducting medium. Sound is collected by the external ear, called the pinna, detected by the tympanic membrane of the eardrum, and transmitted to three small ossicle bones, the malleus (hammer), incus (anvil), and stapes (stirrup). The stapes vibrates the oval window of the cochlea, which is filled with fluid that then moves and is in turn detected by tiny hair cells that transmits the information to a sensory dendrite connected to the auditory nerve. In other words, sound is created by molecular motion.

It is measured by two criteria: frequency, or pitch, and amplitude, or volume. Frequency is a measurement of how fast the molecules move, and amplitude is how far they move. There are few theoretical limits on either. There are sounds beyond the range of a normal human's hearing ability. A dog whistle, for instance, emits a sound at an ultrasonic frequency. Some animals can sense subsonic frequencies as well. This is due to shorter and longer hairs in the cochlea that vibrate to the shorter and longer waves of ultra- and sub- sonic frequencies, or perhaps special sensing organs in some animals. Perhaps Wolverine has both shorter and longer hairs in his cochlea and so can sense ultra- and sub- sonic frequencies of sound.

The ultrasonic range of sound has many unusual properties. It can be used for medical imaging as a harmless substitute for X-rays. Like radar and sonar, the ultrasound bounces back off objects and a sensing device then translates that information into detailed images. Medical technology has utilized this concept to provide the first photos of fetuses in the womb via ultrasound. At higher—which is to say louder—amplitudes, ultrasound causes actual temperature fluctuations—i.e. heating—and is used to warm internal muscles in a form of massage in physical therapy.

VELOCITY OF SOUND

The speed of sound in dry air at the freezing point (0° Celsius or 32° Farenheit) is 331.6 meters per second (740 miles per hour). This speed is also known as Mach 1, after the Austrian scientist Ernst Mach, who measured it. The velocity of sound is affected by heat and media. If the temperature goes up, the speed goes up, too. And the more solid the media, the faster the sound transmission. In water, sound travels at 1,402.3 meters per second or 4,600 feet per second at 0° C. In steel, sound travels at 5,060 meters per second at 0° C.

TASTE

There are only four receptors: one each for sweet, sour, salt, and bitter. Taste is a chemical sense, like smell. A lot of what we taste depends on smell, which heavily modifies what we put in our mouths. The tongue is covered with bumps called "papillae" which contain taste buds. The buds contain receptor cells from which hair-like cilia, or microvilli, extend. Microvilli transform chemical properties into electrochemical properties. Humans have fewer taste buds than most other animals. Perhaps Wolverine has a more animal-like tongue. He might also have more area in his hindbrain devoted to taste-processing, as the four basic tastes don't add up to a million different flavors unless your brain is able to recognize discrete combinations of proportions.

The four basic taste receptors are found, mostly, in different places in the mouth. Sweet and salty receptors tend to be concentrated on the tip of the tongue. Sour receptors are concentrated on the sides of the tongue. Bitter receptors are concentrated way back in the throat and up on the roof of the mouth, the soft palate above the tongue. But there are some of all types of receptors scattered all over. Any lover of hard candies knows that it's fun to tuck them under one side of the back of the tongue and then the other.

SMELL: THE OLFACTORY SYSTEM

The sense of smell, or olfactory sense, is perhaps the most complicated of the human senses. It might have been the first to evolve, and is certainly very closely tied to memory, perhaps more so than other senses. We all know how certain odors can evoke powerful memories. The average human being, it is said, can recognize up to 10,000 separate scents. Smell can not only detect separate odors but, in conjunction with taste, can synthesize different scents into one impression. It can also produce strong visceral physical responses: the smell of rotten meat can, for example, induce vomiting. On a more pleasant note, pheromones can attract a potential mate.

MUCOSA AND EPITHELIUM

The nose collects odors and the molecules with scent are drawn to the hair-like cilia of receptors in the two olfactory mucosa, which are five-centimeter-square surfaces. There is one in each nasal passage. These cilia stick out of the tops of neurons and into the mucosa, which is a thin layer of mucus on the surface of the cell. There are at least 10 cilia per neuron and they are located in the epitheliums.

The two olfactory epitheliums are deep down on each side of the nose. They are located behind a quick turn at the top of the nasal cavity, just below the level of the eyes. Each epithelium is only a few centimeters square but has about five million neurons, not to mention their supporting cells and stem cells. Conceivably, a larger epithelium would aid a higher odor detection rate. This might be part of the reason that Wolverine has greater sensitivity to odors.

In the epitheliums, neurons that comprise a given odor receptor don't cluster together but, rather, are randomly distributed within certain broad regions called expression zones. The cilia of the receptors are excited by chemical interactions with an odor's molecules. Each neuron has a long fiber, or axon, that sticks through a tiny opening in the bone above it, the cribriform plate, to make a connection, or synapse, with other neurons in the olfactory bulb. Once the axons get to the olfactory bulb, they're no longer randomly organized. They re-assort themselves so that all those expressing the same receptor cluster together on the same place in the olfactory bulb.

This makes for a very organized diagram of olfactory information received from different receptors. It also allows the brain read the information like map coordinates. If it sees activity in specific positions on the olfactory bulb, it knows that those correspond to specific odor receptors which, in turn, respond to specific scents. The bulb is on top of a bone—remember that cribriform plate?—that is on top of the mucosa. It's a pea-sized structure right under the brain's frontal lobe and is technically part of the brain. The bulb sends signals to the brain's limbic system.

If Wolverine has a larger epithelium he might also need a larger portion of his brain's limbic system to map the additional axons' signals to the olfactory bulb. The limbic system also controls many aspects of emotion, which might be why smells can elicit such affective memories. From the limbic system, the signals go to the frontal cortex, which is the thinking part of the brain. There, we can mull over why the scent of bubble gum and eraser chalk reminds us so much of our first love in grade school.

There are probably between 500 and 1,000 separate receptor proteins in the olfactory neurons. That's one percent of the genome. This means that one out of every 100 genes is likely to be engaged in the detection of odors. This huge number of genes reflects the crucial importance of this sense, and is one of the reasons why we can recognized about 10,000 different scents. Wolverine, with his highly developed sense of smell, might have even more genes involved in this process.

TOUCH

The pressure-sensitive whorls on our fingertips are so sensitive we can feel the individual colored silk threads embedded into the rag paper of the U.S. dollar bill. We can feel things almost as small as we can see. Our touch resolution is better than one-hundredth of an inch. And our faces are almost as sensitive as our fingertips, because that's where we keep all our other sense organs.

We tend to lead with our heads, and use our faces to feel important environmental factors such as wind pressure and temperature. We have far fewer touch receptors on our backs. Try touching two fingers, about an inch apart, to someone's bare back. If you can get someone to let you do this you might be surprised to find that they have trouble telling you if they're being touched with one finger or two.

Touch might be considered both the fifth and sixth sense in that it's actually a number of different senses. It is detected by receptors in the minute structures that lie on hair-like nerve fibers in the skin. There are at least six different kinds of round, coin-shaped receptors. Each type registers one sensation: vibration, light touch, pressure, pain, cold, and heat. Heat and cold receptors generally follow the range of ideal survival conditions for animal life—from the freezing point of water to its boiling point. Anything above or below is moot. Once you reach the danger point, it all feels awful. Heat receptors probably don't encode into memory as well as smell or sight, which is why we can't remember how cold it was last year at Thanksgiving but we do remember the pumpkin pie.

The fact that heat and cold are separate senses registered by separate receptors explains why we can feel both hot and cold at the same time. A fever will produce that sensation. Or, if you abruptly stick your hand into a bath water of an extreme in temperature, it may take a moment to sort out if it's very hot or very cold. Internal organ receptors deal with touch, vibration, temperature, and pain.

The external skin, or cutaneous, touch receptors pick up sensations outside the body. Internal receptors register sensations within. These are called somesthetic senses.

Vestibular senses detect balance, orientation, and gravity. In the semicircular canals of the ears, hair cells along three planes respond to shifts of liquid within the cochlea and provide a three-dimensional sense of equilibrium, while calcium carbonate crystals can shift in response to gravity and provide sensory information about gravity and acceleration. Finally, kinesthetic senses use receptors in the muscles and joints to detect body position and movement. Wolverine has all of his senses enhanced. There is room for more of all these receptors, but increasing them also means increasing pain perception.

If we felt the pain of every pressure on our feet as keenly as we felt things on our faces, we pedestrians would be in agony all the time. However, the natural opiates of the brain respond to pain and a balance could be struck between deadening of pain and heightening of perception. There are also purely psychological mechanisms that deal with pain. Some people have higher pain thresholds than others, and Wolverine would definitely fit into the "high pain threshold" category.

OTHER SENSES

There is a lot of speculation about senses beyond those linked with the five types of receptors. People have many unexplained sensations and some theorists have considered extra senses as explanations. Some research has tended to support—or, at the very least, not contradicted—these theories. These other senses might not only account for some of Wolverine's increased perception, but many of the extrasensory perceptions exhibited by other mutants.

The pineal gland might somehow be responsible foe some of the following senses:

A *time sense* which perceives and accurately anticipates the daily motions of the sun and the monthly motions of the moon. This might be due to a deeply ingrained physical memory of cycles of light and darkness.

A *disaster sense* which perceives coming earthquakes and storms. This might be due to sensitivity to solar and lunar rhythms, solar flares and sunspots, and moon-caused tidal changes in both water and solid ground.

A high-band visual sense which perceives frequencies beyond those we normally see.

Cutaneous senses are based on receptors in the skin which perceive balance and imbalance regarding what is external to the bio-body, occasionally at some astonishing distances, and motion outside the body, even when the body is asleep.

Given Wolverine's extraordinary tracking ability, it's entirely possible that he has an organ that is a non-visual wave motion-detector that perceives non-visual oscillating patterns, magnetic fields, infrared radiation, electrical energy, geoelectromagnetic pulses, magnetic fields—especially biological ones—and local and distant heat sources of heat. It is possible that he has senses capable of receiving and transmitting all sorts of information. These senses might have receptors in the endocrine and neuropeptide systems which perceive directional and location and/or the eyes which perceive radiation such as X-rays, cosmic rays, infrared radiation, and ultraviolet light. Possibly, Wolverine can even perceive differences in pressure and electromagnetic frequencies.

ADAMANTIUM

One cannot talk about Wolverine without discussing the amazing steel alloy known as adamantium. Adamantium has the characteristics of the heaviest metals, and is most likely an alloy containing at least one heavy metal. It's important to note that heaviness and density do not always make for hardness. Glass, which is a crystalline form of the light element silicon, is very hard. So too is ice, the crystalline form of water, which is made from the very light elements hydrogen and oxygen.

Crystallinity, which is determined by a specific geometric molecular organization, can make for harder materials. Steel is very hard but unlike glass and ice, it is also flexible, so it does not shatter. Basic steel is made from iron and carbon heated and mixed together. It has a somewhat crystalline structure. Hardness, by the way, depends largely on the stability of the molecular structure. If all the atoms fit together snugly, bonded by perfectly matching electrical valence, it takes a lot of physical force to knock them apart. Alloys are mixtures of different elements. If the valences are right and the elements are tossed together in the right way, they can form a new, stable compound. Sometimes it takes a chemical catalyst to trigger this formation. In addition to the inclusion of measured amounts of other metals, it takes pressure and heat, of specific temperatures for specific times, to make various kinds of steel. Medieval Japanese blacksmiths had secret songs they would sing when making what were the toughest swords in the world. The length of the songs determined the lengths of time to heat and cool the strips of steel they hammered.

All objects are affected to some degree by magnetism. Nuclear Magnetic Resonance Imaging (NMRI) utilizes this fact to create medical images. But adamantium is obviously far more magnetic than human flesh, or the magnetic force that Magneto employed to yank it out of Wolverine would have pulled all of his body apart, not just the metal portion.

It is interesting to note that the only thing that can cut apart adamantium is a certain type of particle beam. Given the hardness of adamantium, it is conceivable that it would retain its stability and cohesion even when shaved to molecular thickness. Were one to make steel claws this sharp, they wouldn't remain so for long: the edges would abrade and become dull. This is obviously not the case for Wolverine's adamantium claws. They might be thin enough to slice grooves of molecular thinness. No wonder he can hack up just about anything! If you can start with a little molecule-thin cut on a hunk of rock or metal then you should be able to quickly saw right through it, for at the molecular level, even the toughest substances are susceptible to getting trimmed.

QUICKSILVER

Pietro Maximoff is the world's fastest mutant. Quicksilver and his twin sister Wanda (see Scarlet Witch) are both the offspring of Erik Magnus Lehnsherr (see Magneto) and his gypsy wife, Magda.

The first-born daughter of Erik and Magda Lehnsherr died tragically. Eric used his mutant powers to kill the people who caused the child's death. Magda was horrified; both by his powers and the mad megalomania he displayed. She was essentially a simple gypsy woman and this was far outside of her ability to comprehend, so she fled.

To make matters worse, she found that she was pregnant. She traveled alone through harsh weather and rough terrain of the Balkan Mountains in the small nation of Transia. She climbed up the rocky trails until she came across Wundagore, the citadel of an apostate scientist who, like Dr. Moreau, accelerated the evolution of beasts so that they reached a plane of intelligence similar to humans. There she found refuge. A bizarre cow-woman was midwife to the birth of Magda's children, who she named Wanda and Pietro.

Magda's postpartum depression combined with her fear that should her mad husband find her, he would kill both her and her children. Convinced she was a lethal liability to her babies, she went out onto the mountain, to die in the winter snows.

The infants were given to a pair of gypsies who raised Wanda and Pietro as their own. In their early adolescence, the twins discovered they had special powers and were forced to flee the gypsies. For the next few years, they wandered central Europe and lived off the land.

Professor Charles Xavier learned of their existence and tried to recruit them into the X-Men, the new team he was forming to protect mutants. In fact, they were among the first mutants he approached. However, they rebuffed his attempts, longing for normal lives in which they could hide their mutant powers. Unfortunately, this was not to be.

One day Wanda's uncontrollable hex powers caused a house to burst into flame and some villagers happened to spot her in action. An angry mob soon formed. Magneto saved them from the mob and asked them to join him. Not knowing that this man was their father who had driven their mother to suicide, the siblings joined Magneto and became founding members of his Brotherhood of Evil Mutants.

The association soon soured. For a time the twins continued to serve Magneto out of a sense of debt, as well as fear of his temper, so much like Pietro's. Finally, they found the courage to switch sides, but instead of taking Xavier up on his proposition, they joined the world-renowned super hero team, the Avengers. The move made headlines. While the Scarlet Witch has maintained her membership with the Avengers, Quicksilver did not. Impatient, tempermental, Quicksilver has led a tumultuous life, most of it of his own making.

POWERS

Nonetheless, Quicksilver has impressive abilities. He can move at extraordinary speed and has the physiology needed to support this. What's more, Quicksilver possesses superhuman strength, especially in his lower body. This is part of the adaptations necessary for his inhumanly speedy movement, particularly his running. With his upper body, he can lift approximately a ton. He can leg-press at least that much. In fact, it's been reported that he's capable of lifting ten times that amount.

Quicksilver's entire body is oriented toward the rigors of high-speed running. This means that his cardiovascular and respiratory systems are many times more efficient than those of normal humans. Quicksilver metabolizes an estimated 95% of the caloric energy of foodstuffs as compared to the normal human use of just 25%.

His joints are smoother and lubricated far more efficiently than those of humans, and his tendons have the tensile strength of spring steel. His bones contain materials considerably more durable than calcium, and can withstand the dynamic shocks of his feet touching the ground at speeds of over 100 miles per hour.

His practical reaction time is about five times faster than that of any human, and the speed at which his brain processes information is commensurate with his bodily speed, enabling him to perceive his surroundings as he travels at high velocities.

The chemical processes of his musculature are so highly enhanced that his body doesn't generate fatigue poisons, the normal byproducts of locomotion, which force the body to rest. Rather, Quicksilver constantly expels waste products through exhalation during his accelerated respiration.

Salty secretions from the lachrymal (tear) glands lubricating his eyes are thicker and stickier than nonmutants', preventing evaporation and resulting friction from eroding his eyeballs as he runs. The same mutant secretions keep his joints moving with frictionless efficiency. Perhaps the structure of his joints differ from those of normal humans, resembling ball-bearing or roller-bearing parts in machinery.

Quicksilver's top speed is 175 mph, approximately three times faster than that of the fastest land animal, the cheetah. He's dodged machine gun fire, and by racing in a ten-foot diameter circle he can create cyclone-like gusts of wind that will knock a man off his feet.

Given a 500-foot approach to gain momentum, he can run up the side of a building to the height of 300 feet before gravity overtakes him. Quicksilver can literally run upon water. With a 100-foot approach for momentum, he can cross approximately 1000 feet—thanks to surface tension—before beginning to sink. Quicksilver has sufficient energy resources to enable him to run at 175 mph for about four hours.

The extent of his physical durability is unknown. Obviously, he has immense capacity to withstand air resistance and friction generated by moving at such high velocities. His metabolism and endurance allow him to be immune to most fatigue poisons as well as heal his injuries much faster than normal.

GENETIC ORIGINS

Our speed is limited by a number of physical factors including muscle tone, metabolic speed, and energy resources. Other species with different genetic heritages are not so limited. In fact, most animals have better physical resources than we do. We put a lot of metabolic energy into thinking and just being conscious 16 hours per day. Few animals are as active as we are. Most predators, for instance, sleep almost 20 hours per day. Not only does inferior muscle tone make humans weaker than most animals, it also makes them slower. Were we to have the muscle tone of a cheetah, we would be able to run at speeds of up to 70 mph—for limited distances. As it is, a four-minute mile is considered remarkable for us human slow pokes.

THE IMPORTANCE OF FRICTION

It's amazing that Quicksilver isn't worn away to a nubbin by his fancy footwork. His body must be durable indeed, for friction is his enemy just as much, if not moreso, than any living enemy.

Friction is the force that appears whenever an object moves through air, water, etc., or rubs against another object. Friction opposes motion. Heat and sound are the byproducts of friction, and indicate that friction is robbing energy from some movement or endeavor.

It's impossible to have movement without friction here on Earth. Only in the vacuum of space is it possible to avoid friction—provided that you also avoid collisions with meteors, etc. Quicksilver must be able to defeat the laws of physics as we know them in order to produce silent, heatless speed. The heat generated by his feet coming in contact with the ground alone would most likely set small fires (talk about a hot foot!).

Oddly enough, the one place where he needs to maintain friction is the bottom of his feet. Just as car tires provide steering—and traction—by gripping the road under all weather conditions, so must Quicksilver's feet maintain friction with the ground, enabling him to control his direction. We can only assume that the soles of Quicksilver's footwear is made from an extremely durable material.

ENERGY INTAKE AND SINGULARITIES

The energy involved is another consideration. Quicksilver's caloric intake to fuel that much movement would be enormous. Nevertheless, we rarely see Quicksilver eating. How does he gain the energy from which to maintain his momentum?

David Hilbert, as previously noted, is the German mathematician who wrote about multi-dimensional possibilities almost a century ago. His picture of things is that there are virtually an infinite number of dimensions and that our universe exists in about 12 of them. We puny humans only perceive three and a half dimensions (the half being our perception of time in which we can only move one way).

But some subatomic particles, particularly the devious tachyon, are suspected of traveling backwards in time. So, if tachyons can do it, why can't certain mutants do it?

Therefore, Quicksilver may have the capacity to lift himself out of our own limited dimensional plane, shift forward in time, and jump back into our reality, giving the illusion of tremendous speed. If he ducks in and out every hundred microseconds, the illusion given would be that he is here constantly. Quicksilver might be able to push and pull himself out of a dimension-warping radius which is activated by quantum level forces.

CONTROLLABLE SINGULARITIES

So how does a guy go about hopping in and out of dimensional planes? An awful lot of these X-Men seem to have access to doorways to either other, non-Einsteinian universe or to other dimensions.

Using Occam's Razor again, let's assume they all have the same method. The only known way to get out of our universe and our dimensional planes is with what is variously called an Einstein-Rosen Bridge, a mathematical singularity, a wormhole, and, most popularly, a black hole. In the entry for Jean Grey, we considered the possibility of containing and controlling a mini-black hole. We proposed some quantum level chain reactions that might in theory do the trick. The thought along these lines is that the hole isn't in the mutant's head in the conventional sense. Rather it is skewed dimensionally so that its event horizon is safely distant from the mutant cranium yet close enough that its unique properties can be accessed by properly equipped mutants. If the hole were curled up in one of our tinier dimensions, then a mutant might be able to access its effects from our third dimension while remaining unaffected by the hole's event horizon. This might enable a dimension-hopper (and quantum force manipulator) like Quicksilver to push and pull himself in and out of its dimension-warping radius. What looks like speed to us is just a mutant playing hide-and-seek with quantum forces.

RELATIVISTIC AGING

It's been said that Quicksilver lives a hundred years for every one of ours. Evidently he doesn't age much, if that is the case. Even though Quicksilver cannot go the speed of light, let's have some fun imagining what it would be like if he could.

There is actually a way to live a hundred years without aging, and it does require speeding up—but by speeding up, you slow down. This is the condition described by Einstein's special theory of relativity.

The theory has it that if you could fly at speeds nearing that of light, time would slow down for you. You would age one year while the rest of the universe aged a hundred years. Sound familiar? That's a stock plot of a lot of old sci-fi stories. The Lorentz-FitzGerald contraction equation implies fantastic things happen as you approach the speed of light.

So as Quicksilver speeds up, his personal timeframe slows down. If he spends an hour racing at relativistic speeds, it would seem like less than a minute to him.

Now, let's reverse the situation, and speed up the rest of the universe to relativistic speeds or slow Quicksilver's relativistic timeframe. Quicksilver would appear to be moving very quickly, as if he were in a fast-motion film ... but the rest of the universe would whiz by and leave him far behind.

That's the paradox of Special Relativity. The faster you go, the slower you seem to go and vice versa. Under this paradox, the physical motions of a star traveler flying at the speed of light would be so slow as to be undetectable, whereas our motions would appear to him as a blur of speed.

How would we look to Quicksilver? It depends upon your relativistic point of view. Most likely, to him the entire world is moving in slow motion—yet all around him are aging rapidly, while he, forever young, is the only one moving at the proper speed.

BLOB

Fred J. Dukes was actually a "carnie," a carnival performer, before he became an adversary of the X-Men. Blob was one of the X-Men's earliest enemies and has never been definitively defeated. Over the years he's returned time and again to take on each new team of X-Men. He has withstood not just Cyclops' power beam but Colossus' punches and Wolverine's adamantium claws as well.

Given his surly personality, you wouldn't consider Blob to be a "team player" but he's been a loyal member of at least five different versions of the mutant team that has been one of the X-Men's most enduring adversaries, the Brotherhood of Evil Mutants. What's more, with his reputation you might not think of him as a good guy, but he has actually been on the right side of the law. He was a member of Freedom Force, the government organization charged to oversee superhuman activities. Unsavory he may be, but Blob is also interesting and unpredictable.

MASS AND GRAVITY CONTROL

Blob can increase his density until he is virtually immovable. His big plump body has great mass, strength, resilience, and indestructibility. A normal person who was this heavy would be termed "morbidly obese" by doctors but in the case of Blob, this not only seems to be a healthy state of affairs for him but, in fact, absolutely desirable.

When he escaped jail to join the second grouping of the Brotherhood of Evil Mutants, Blob demonstrated that he had learned how to increase his personal gravitational pull by concentrating his mass.

He can become virtually immovable at will, as long as he is in contact with the ground. He does this by binding himself to the earth beneath him in much the same manner as did the giant wrestler Antaeus of Libya, offspring of Poseidon and Demeter, who opposed Hercules in the Greek myths.

This binding effect creates a unidirectional increase of gravity beneath Blob. This gravity field stretches out to approximately five feet around him from his center of gravity. If there is enough power to uproot him, it also uproots the ground beneath him in an area corresponding to the radius of the field. By extreme concentration, Blob can broaden the field beneath him even farther.

The fat tissues beneath his skin are able to absorb the impact of bullets, artillery shells, and even missiles. The larger projectiles bounce from his body at half the force of impact. The smaller ones, imbedded in the layers of his fat tissue, can be ejected when Blob flexes his muscles.

Blob might have some upper limit to his ability to absorb impact but so far no force has reached that threshold. He could survive a head-on collision with a bus traveling at a hundred miles an hour. Such a meteorite would weigh more than half a million *tons* and would be super-heated from its atmospheric descent. One wonders what sort of impact would be required to flatten Blob. In addition to being virtually immovable, he has an extraordinarily high tolerance to pain. Catastrophic assaults never cause him to so much as wince.

The fat tissue of his epidermis is resilient enough to return to its usual shape in a few seconds after attack. His skin cannot be severed, cut, frostbitten, or devastated by any skin disease, due in part to the skin's great flexibility and extraordinary durability and in part to the hugely accelerated rate at which his skin and tissues regenerate. However, he does have one weakness: heat. Excessive heat can severely debilitate him.

FAT AND GENETICS

The amount of body fat a person has is determined by two factors: environment and genetics. Some people are plump because they work in jobs that don't demand much physical exercise and they have easy access to too much food. And example of this can be seen in most parts of the United States, which has the most overweight people of any culture in the world. That includes several cultures such as Samoa, in the South Pacific, where people routinely tip the scales at a husky 300+ pounds. However, those Samoans aren't overweight: their genes build them on a big scale. Blob must have similar genes to retain so much fat.

The food we eat is converted to blood sugar. Some foods, such as carbohydrates, are more readily converted to blood sugar than others—such as meat proteins—are. For people prone to gaining weight, carbos tend to end up converted to fat deposits rather than metabolized into body energies. Due to variations in genetic disposition, everyone has slightly different blood chemistries, which is one reason why you see so many different body sizes. A professional athlete actually gains a lot of metabolic energy from carbohydrate intake because his physical activities force a fast and efficient conversion of calories.

From what we've seen, Blob's metabolism reacts the same way to all food. He just needs lots of it. But, as you'll see below, food isn't his only source of energy.

DENSITY, MASS, GRAVITY, AND WEIGHT

When density increases, so does mass. Mass plus gravity equals weight. It takes some complicated phenomena to enable Blob's body to continue functioning as if it were lightweight flesh and blood when it has the mass of something beyond even the heaviest elements on the periodic table.

The heaviest elements known are the transuranic elements such as plutonium and americanium. A Blob-sized batch of these ultra-heavy elements would, indeed, be too heavy to budge for your average human—but not your average forklift. (Beast, by way of example, is capable of lifting several tons, but he can't even budge Blob.)

One way for Blob to increase his weight would be to draw matter from *somewhere else* to make himself heavier. One can't just increase one's density out of thin air; protons and neutrons have to be involved at the very least. Blob pulls these in somehow, and thereby manages to get heavier than any known matter.

Of course, he's got to be careful about getting *too* heavy. If he should reach a mass equivalent to three of our suns, he'll collapse into a black hole. But at the moment he's a long way from that. He's even a fair distance from what is called "collapsed matter," the pre-black hole state of burned-out suns known as brown dwarfs whose electrons have been stripped away. All that's left are protons and neutrons collapsing inward, drawn by their own weight, into compact, ultra-dense matter that some call neutronium.

EXOTIC BIOCHEMISTRY

Blob *is* very heavy, so heavy that one wonders how he can keep his eyelids up, expand his lungs to breathe, pump his blood to . . . well, to be blunt, *live*. Ordinary non-mutant human flesh and blood would never survive Blob's sort of weight gain, much less maintain normal operations. Something must enable Blob to stay alive and active.

He started out as a normal-appearing kid. Upon the onset of puberty and the activation of his mutant X-genes, perhaps an organic cold fusion process took place early in his adolescent development that created molecules of exotic matter within him. These molecules might function much like normal organic carbon-hydrogen-oxygen-nitrogen molecules but because of their mutant configuration have exotic properties necessary for Blob's physiology to support itself.

Non-mutant, but no less exotic, life forms already exist on Earth in some of the most hostile environments imaginable. These exotic life forms are known as extremophiles and they live in infernal places. Sulfolobus and Crenarchaeota thrive in the near-boiling hot sulfur pools in Yellowstone National Park and black smokers live in the deep sea volcanic vents on the ocean floor. Additionally, after an Apollo mission returned with artifacts from the Apollo 12 lunar mission, NASA discovered that one of the Apollo 12 cameras contained a still-living microscopic stowaway, *streptoccocus mitis*. This bacteria survived a stay of almost three years on the Moon.

While these organisms cannot manipulate their mass like Blob, it is important to understand that life has demonstrated that it can exist under extreme conditions. Blob's physiology is extreme. The mutant X-genes have, amongst other things, made such existence possible in a higher organism.

GRAVITONS

Blob can increase his gravitational pull by increasing his mass. Normally only mass produces gravity. Okay, so how can Blob focus his gravitational mass? Some theoreticians believe that there is a fundamental particle that propagates gravity, just as electricity is propagated by electrons. Electricity is made of electrons. Gravity might therefore be composed of gravitons. Sadly, the theorists' pals, the particle accelerator researchers, have not yet found evidence of such a particle. That does not mean it does not exist. Until Anton van Leeuwenhoek examined a drop of water with his new invention, the simple microscope, no one knew single-cell life existed. For decades everyone thought that the smallest particles of matter were the subatomic particles protons, neutrons and electrons. As technology advanced, scientists discovered those were merely the largest. So it is entirely possible that we have not achieved the level of technology needed to find the graviton that the theorists claim exists. (By the way, attempts to confirm or disprove the theoretical existence of the graviton is not the only baffling problem scientists confront in the study of gravity. It may surprise you but there is a lot about gravity that scientists don't understand.) Blob could have some sort of bodily system resembling our own nervous system, but instead of conducting chemical exchanges and electrical charges, the exotic matter that makes up his mass would carry gravitons.

Assuming that Blob can attract or generate and control gravitons, this would not only explain his ability to increase his weight, it would also explain how he could function when his weight would otherwise be heavy enough to collapse his lungs and internal organs—in other words, kill him.

Additionally, he wouldn't need to increase his mass at all; he would only need to increase his gravity. Bear in mind that normally, gravity is an effect of mass and cannot exist without it. However, if the theoretical graviton does exist, then spectacular effects would be possible without any mass.

Blob's power makes him the classical immovable object. One can't resist wondering what would happen if he met up with Juggernaut, the living embodiment of an equally absolute and infinitely irresistible force. All we can say for certain is that it would be best to witness that event from a safe distance, like the Moon, because the impact could truly be earthshaking.

ANGEL

Had his mother been named Leda, instead of Kathryn, and his father Zeus, and not Warren Worthington II, then at least we would have a better idea of who was responsible for the "accident of birth" that blessed Angel with his wings. Yet, while less romantic, the genetic "what" behind the origin of Warren Worthington III's wings is no less fantastic.

One of the original members of the X-Men, Angel is also the richest. Born in Centerport, Long Island, the young Worthington was raised in the prep school tradition of old money. By all accounts, his childhood was happy and (with respect to his social status) as normal as that of any human kid. Handsome, athletic and charming, he had all the earmarks of someone who would be going places. Not until adolescence did his genetic secret reveal itself and change the course of his life.

It was while attending an exclusive boarding school and prior to enrollment at Professor Xavier's School for Gifted Youngsters that puberty struck and Warren Worthington III's perfect world became . . . different.

In short, he grew wings. Within a few months, his new appendages had reached their full length and he could fly. Of course, being a teenager, instead of thinking of how great this was, Worthington could only focus on one thing—that he was a freak. He did what he could to hide his "deformity," including using straps and a harness to hold his wings into place underneath his clothes.

Yet adolescent angst did not completely overwhelm the thrill he had for his genetic gift. Flight has been a dream of mankind since we first saw birds and envied them their freedom of motion. Warren took to flight with the intense enthusiasm of an air force fighter jock. In flight he found he had not only a freedom of motion, but a freedom from his worries and cares. While his wings were unstrapped and he flew through the open air, he was no longer an earthbound student but an Angel of the skies. In a foretaste of his future, and his first act of *noblesse oblige*, he constructively channeled his fear and frustrations and selflessly became the teenaged crime-fighter, Avenging Angel.

Fortunately for the history of the X-Men, this was a short-lived career. He was soon approached by Scott Summers and Robert Drake of Professor Xavier's School for Gifted Youngsters. They revealed their knowledge of his gift. Warren convinced his parents to transfer him to Professor Xavier's "even more exclusive" School for Gifted Youngsters. There he met Henry McCoy and Jean Grey and became a part of the original the X-Men.

The rest is Marvel Universe history.

HUMAN FLIGHT AND GENETIC ENGINEERING

Angel has wings with a 16-foot span. Their extremely flexible structure allows him to fold them (not without some discomfort) against his back, leaving only a bulge beneath his clothing.

Fully extended, Angel's wings are strong enough to allow him to fly while carrying up to 200 pounds of extra weight. He's capable of diving at speeds of 180 miles per hour but his average air speed is 50–70 mph. Given a decent tail wind, he can do better.

Let's cut to the chase here. It's a wonderful dream—one that mankind has had throughout recorded history, and probably since the dawn of humanity. But, will it ever be possible for people to grow wings? Advances in genetic research suggest that yes, *perhaps* someday, normal humans could grow wings using their own genetic makeup.

To make a winged man, in theory then, you would merely have to reprogram and re-deploy his DNA, the basic developmental toolbox that all animals share. In other words, as *ScienceNow*, the daily news web site of *Science Magazine*, reported in an article on genetic examination of eyespot location in butterflies, "...the evolution of new features doesn't require the evolution of new genes or pathways, just a change in how those pathways are used."

Before you start making an appointment with your HMO's primary caregiver so that you can visit that new specialist, the aviaologist, it's probably safe to say in advance that there's no way any HMO is going to pay for it. Also, there's a long way to go before we know for sure whether or not humans really can produce wings. Even then, producing wings won't be easy. The huge amount of human DNA involved shows how daunting a task it would be in even finding the right genomes (a genome is the complete genetic blueprint of a species) to "tickle awake."

Different body plans (and Angel's body would require a lot of modifications in the blueprint) are determined fundamentally by a special group of genes called the "homebox" or HOX genes. They direct the master body plan and switch on and off whole sets of other genes—some to make building blocks, some to regulate other genetic functions. So, assuming that you found the right genes and put them in the right sequence, you might still fail because the HOX genes determined that the sequence did not happen at the biologically right time. Given the dramatic change in physiology that wing growth produces, it's in keeping that it would occur simultaneously with the other major body changes that happen during puberty, the body's preprogrammed transition from juvenile to adult.

Of course, Angel throws us an additional physiological curve. As a mammal, you'd expect that his wings would resemble those of his fellow mammal, the bat. They don't. Instead of leathery skin, his wings have feathers and structurally they appear to resemble the wings of birds. Also, his wings are two *extra* limbs that are attached to his back between the shoulders and spine. We'll be covering the possible makeup of his feathers later. As for how his wings move, perhaps some of his back muscles are working them in an arrangement similar to that of a flying insect, but that—and his six limbs—is where any further resemblance he has to the insect family ends.

AVIAN MORPHOLOGY

Even though a bird's bones are hollow and light compared to human bones, a 16-foot set of bird's wings would still weigh over 20 pounds, hollow bones or not. Yet Angel only weighs about 150 pounds total. Subtract 20 pounds for the wings, and he's literally a featherweight at six feet tall. Hollow bones alone wouldn't account for his unusual lightness of being. Perhaps his bones' structure is also composed of something a bit lighter and tougher than pure calcium. This would mean that Angel is a mutant right down to his bones. Certainly he would have to be if he ever hoped to get off the ground.

From these observations, we can assume certain things.

Angel's wings are lightweight and made of an unusual material that collapses unnaturally.

The muscles that control and power his wings, like all of Beast's musculature (see Beast entry) are unusually strong. However, the problem here is that normally the stronger the muscle, the denser and heavier the material.

Using Occam's Razor we seek to find one answer for two questions. We must hypothesize a material that is lightweight, strong, and collapsible.

Carbon composites (cross-fibered epoxy-resin) construction would do the trick. This is a material where very thin layers of lightweight carbon fibers are set into epoxy resin, like fiberglass. They are epoxied together in layers with the grain of each layer running in a different direction. This gives the material the strength and flexibility of a metal such as aluminum, but a fraction of the weight. And such a material could easily be designed in collapsible sections. Carbon-based synthetic materials show potential for stronger, lighter qualities than the silicon fibers in commercial use. Also, unlike silicon, carbon, along with hydrogen, oxygen, and nitrogen (CHON), makes up the basic components of life.

Carbon has an atomic structure that allows it to bond to almost anything and form a seemingly endless series of compositions, among them, plastics. Broadly speaking, plastic is created from the sludge that remains after gasoline has been distilled out of crude oil. This sludge is catalyzed with additives to create the raw materials for the various manufactured plastics that we take for granted today. In particular, and more to the point, light, strong, durable and flexible carbon fibers are one such result.

In some manner, Angel's genes might produce a carbon-based, entirely organic material that is structurally analogous to cross-fibered resin epoxy. This is not entirely far-fetched, as we have some "designer genes" producing marketable commodities already.

Although such materials as cross-fibered epoxy resin do not exist in nature today, they might one day. The current advances in the Human Genome Project—the mapping of the entire gene structure of human DNA—will lead us eventually to the capability of designing human genes to produce a variety of results. This could eliminate some types of cancer and other genetically based diseases. It could lengthen the human life span, as has already been done with flies by the work of physicist and genetic specialist Seymour Benzer. This would take an awful lot of genetic design since there is no "wing gene" that we can simply turn "on."

METABOLISM

Angel has absolutely no body fat. It's all muscle, baby! Since an average healthy human has a minimum of 20 percent fat, that's a lot of extra muscle. That's an important advantage for a flying man but it comes at a cost for it must make him a lot less human than he appears.

His physiology must be very different than ours because most of us would have trouble surviving without body fat. We use body fat to insulate us, and even with that insulation, we'd have trouble surviving at the low temperatures of sustained flight. It gets colder the higher you go but the real threat of cold comes from the chilling wind one encounters when flying quickly through cold air masses. (Think of meteorologists' "wind chill factor" warnings on blustery winter days.) The acceleration of the metabolism in flight would require reserves of body fat to use for energy. Angel's body must have access to a source of energy to both warm him and to power his flight. It wouldn't seem likely that metabolic resources could sustain this level of activity.

So what keeps Angel warm and gives him his "get-up-and-go"? There is the possibility that he literally "eats like a bird"—which, contrary to popular belief, means to be extraordinarily voracious—ingesting twice his body weight every day, like a hummingbird, in order to obtain the energy necessary for his flights. That would scarcely leave him any time for doing anything else. And, as you've probably noticed, in all of his adventures you rarely see him eating. Therefore, we must assume that not only does he make extraordinarily efficient in his use of energy, he probably has an "alternative energy source." The only other part of his body that is sufficiently exposed to the elements to make such a thing practical is his wings, specifically, his feathers. It's entirely possible that Angel's "feathers" are actually a form of storage battery or solar cell wherein he is able to trap and contain energy (constantly replenished by the sun's rays). Leaves of deciduous trees perform a similar energy-gathering function, and are so efficient and cheap to produce that when cold weather comes and the tree goes dormant, it sheds its leaves and regenerates new ones the following spring.

Manufactured solar cells—called photovolaic cells in technical circles—are semiconductor diodes. The more efficient ones are made with indium phosphide and gallium arsenide. This is toxic and indium is a relatively scarce element that would be hard to metabolically accumulate. However, silicon can also be used. Silicon is not, of course, a component of any known organic compounds, but we do accumulate large amounts of calcium, another organically inert element, so it is not entirely unfeasible. Silicon is not as efficient as indium phosphide and gallium arsenide and requires a large surface array to generate even modest currents. The layering of the Angel's feathers would provide immensely more surface area than a smooth surface. Given sufficient thinness of feathers and deepness of layering, the surface area could conceivably be exponentially larger. This might indeed collect a fair amount of solar energy.

THE BIOMECHANICS OF FLIGHT

Let's assume that Angel's muscles are unusually lightweight, enabling him to achieve lift off and that his solar-cell feathers provide the energy needed to keep him warm and nourish the muscles that power his wings.

But once in flight, what *keeps* him there? Certainly he doesn't constantly flap his wings as fast as a hummingbird. And yet heavier-than-air individuals must in some way generate sufficient force to overcome their weight and support them in the air.

The beating of wings acts to catch the wind and bear the flier aloft. It also forces air backward, pushing the flier forward. So wings are both support and driving mechanisms. But is it truly necessary to have the wings perform both services? Since his body is more human in design (which is to say *not* aerodynamic) the answer here must be yes—and with help.

Angel has been able to fly and hover in enclosed places.

As anyone who remembers dodging the sparrows in the TWA terminal at Kennedy airport in New York City can say, it's not impossible for birds to do so. But sparrows and parakeets, another bird confined to enclosed spaces, are small. Also they generally don't hover for very long. Angel, on the other hand, has hovered for extended periods of time. So it's not enough to have wings. There's got to be something else.

Cetaceans and other sea mammals, such as walruses and seals, possess special bladders that are used to counteract the effects of the tremendous pressures encountered in deep sea dives and resurfacing. Flying above 5,000 feet, in addition to the problem of extreme cold, places Angel at risk from lower atmospheric pressure and possible oxygen deprivation. To counteract these effects, and to make him aerodynamically buoyant, it's entirely possible that Angel possesses separate flight organs and/or bladders. This would have the advantage of letting his wings act more like stabilizers, allowing him to steer and remain upright, especially in enclosed spaces.

In addition, the flight bladder/s could expand, generating a force reducing or neutralizing his weight so that it becomes equal to the upthrust of his wings. The fact that we've not seen any distension of his body in consequence of using a flight bladder is less a case for him not having them than an indication that he has numerous small ones scattered throughout his body. This would be particularly necessary in his arms and legs, as the muscles in those limbs would quickly tire without some additional means of support.

Modern biology has clearly shown that while such things as Angel's wings are not possible now, neither are they objects forever confined to tales of fantasy and science-fiction. Thanks to the rapid advances already made, the only real question is whether advances that make such genetic manipulations feasible will occur in our generation.

BEAST

Hank McCoy's father was exposed to intense radiation in a nuclear accident. Surprisingly, he suffered no catastrophic ill effects. The only apparent results of the exposure were seen with the birth of his son. Hank was born with unusually big hands and feet. But these were still within the very broad parameters of normalcy, so he wasn't stigmatized. As he developed, it became evident that he had exceptional strength, agility, and dexterity, and a very high level of intelligence. In high school he was a double threat: an exceptional athlete as well as an outstanding scholar.

He was recruited right out of high school to study at Professor Xavier's Academy for Gifted Youngsters. He became one of the original X-Men. There, he took his old nickname from his high school football field as his code name, and became the Beast. Despite his muscular and somewhat thuggish appearance, Hank was actually the intellectual of the group. He continued his studies, focussing on genetic research.

After graduation, he found a position as a genetic researcher and used the opportunity to try to isolate the factor that caused mutations. Perhaps he was looking for a way to alter his genetic makeup to a more normative structure. Despite his exuberant social affect, Hank always wished that he were more normal looking. His Neanderthal-like appearance was very much at odds with his self-image. He was, after all, not a professional wrestler, but a scientific researcher and a good one at that.

Hank got his doctorate in genetics at Xavier's institute and later became an international expert on mutations and evolutionary human biology.

He did manage to isolate the mutating factor but could not reverse it. To the contrary, he was only able to intensify it. At the time, he was conducting a covert investigation on his own, and he decided his serum could help him operate undercover. He used it to temporarily increase his mutation and found himself covered from head to toe with gray fur (which later became blue-black), with fangs, pointed ears, and toes. A happy additional effect was even greater agility and strength. Perhaps, however, he overrated his own scientific abilities, for when he stayed too long in his blue-furred form, he became stuck in it. Now he was even more of a beast than before. It required a bit of adjustment to live in this state 24 hours a day.

Since he is a world-famed geneticist, Hank's time is often taken up with scientific and academic matters. But he still finds time to have an adventure now and then.

His unusually large feet and toes almost have the dexterity of hands and fingers. But his nimbleness is not limited to his feet. He is extremely agile in general, has great physical strength, and can lift up to one ton.

GENETIC ATAVISM

Beast's genetic makeup would seem to have retained some of the ancestral genes that most of us have lost. It's possible that his mutation is what is termed "atavistic," a throwback. However, his blue-furred form implies the presence of some more exotic genes in the mix as well.

Introns are inert material found in DNA. Each of the 10 trillion cells in our body has a complete set of 100,000 genes. Introns take up to 97 percent of that but seem to serve no purpose. There are about a million introns in the DNA of each cell in our bodies. Some scientists theorize that introns are atavistic remnants of older genes. The competing theory is that they came much later. And some believe it's a mixture of both. Before the genes in DNA start to do their work and produce proteins, introns are edited out because they interfere with the process. Eukaryotic cells transcribe the whole DNA sequence, with introns, into RNA. Within the cell nucleus, complexes of enzymes and other proteins (spliceosomes) find and cut out the introns and then splice the RNA back together. Then the RNA leaves the nucleus and goes to a ribosome where it is translated into protein.

Accepted theory has it that introns were originally the connecting elements of the much more primitive genes of early life. Even as connective structures, however, they played a crucial role in genetic organization, for the same type of intron in a different position could create very different structures. Conceivably, if these ancient introns were somehow reactivated, if they were *not* edited out, ancestral traits might result. Possibly this accounts for much of the Beast's appearance.

ATAVISTIC PHYSIOLOGY

Beast has many features that seem to come from our ancestors of millions of years ago. His hairiness, large feet, heavy muscles, physical agility, and tendency to revert to a crouching posture, are all features of earlier models of humanity. In short, Beast is an anachronism. While he has many modern features, such as skull shape, height, and ability to stand upright, much of his skeletal and muscular structure is regressive.

Modern humans have arms and legs of roughly the same length. Beast has longer arms than legs. His ratio of arm-to-leg length is not nearly as extreme as Ramapithecus, our animal-like ancestor but he does have the longer arms of our nearer ancestor, Homo habilus. His leg and foot structure resembles that of our far more recent ancestor, Homo erectus, in that he has a slightly bowlegged posture that forces him to walk more on the outsides of his feet, rather than placing them flatly as we do. His feet have big toes that are arranged at an angle to his other toes, like thumbs. He probably has heavier bones, as erectus did, to anchor his stronger muscles.

Modern humans have weak muscles compared to those of our ape-like ancestors . . . and Beast. He weighs 350 pounds but appears to be the size of a person who weighs a hundred pounds less. This is probably because his muscle mass is more compact than average.

Just as most animals have a greater strength-to-muscle mass ratio than normal humans do, so Beast has superior muscle quality. Chimpanzees (pan troglodytes) rarely stand more than five feet tall but because of their dense muscle mass they weigh around 175 pounds (at that height) and would easily be able to out-wrestle a human of equal weight.

Around 14 million years ago, when our species branched away from apes and chimpanzees, evolutionary processes abandoned the routing of metabolic resources toward the building of compact muscle mass. Our energy goes into other areas such as prolonged activity. Most predators, for instance, are active for only a few hours each day while humans are constantly on the go. Given his physiological makeup, Beast's caloric intake must be at least double that of the rest of us to maintain such a highlevel of energy output on such a continuous basis.

A MODERN BRAIN IN AN APE-LIKE BODY

Beast exhibits characteristics that are considered "neotonous." Neotony is an evolutionary phenomenon that explains why Beast has a big modern head and a muscular hairy body. In neotonous evolution, childlike characteristics become advantageous in the adult and so are retained. A baby chick has a large head, downy feathers, and undersized wings. The ostrich and the moa are example of adult birds with chick-like appearances.

Similarly, modern humans have characteristics of the infants of earlier hominids. A larger head-to-body ratio and hairlessness are notable in the infants of monkeys and apes, which are our closest animal relatives. When the great ancestral forests of Africa died out and humans were pushed onto the grassy plains, larger brains were necessary to figure out how to hunt and survive. Hairlessness helped with cooling the body once we no longer had trees to shade us. In short, we look like the oversized babies of our ancestors while Beast has a distinctly neotonous characteristic: an ape-like body with a larger contemporary head.

BEAST'S PHYSIOLOGY

In some respects Beast's body resembles that of our early ancestor, Ramapithecus, who originated when man and ape first started to diverge. Ramapithecus had muscle tone close to that of an ape or chimpanzee, was hairy, and walked on all fours most of the time. However, their metabolic rates were much lower than Beast's. He would have starved on the ancestral diet.

Beast's posture is a bit closer to that of Australopithecus, who walked upright but wasn't averse to a little knuckle dragging now and then. His brain was also small, and he didn't have the ability to talk.

Homo habilus, the first hominid to walk upright and use stone tools, was hairy, and had the muscle quality of Beast, as well as his pedal dexterity and occasional four-footed posture; however, his head was much smaller than that of modern man-and the Beast. And habilus was much smaller, around the four-foot range. When our ancestors began to use tools and stand upright, they no longer needed animal strength, so habilus wasn't as strong as his ancestors were, but he was still stronger than we are.

There is some speculation as to whether these ancestors had the same vocal apparatus we do, with the larynx sunk back in the throat. If not, they wouldn't have been able to speak vowels, or probably much more than limited animal noises. Despite his inability to talk, habilus might have had something approaching modern intelligence. We know that he could make fires and cook with them. However, current theory has it that the development of language was necessary not merely for communication and cooperation among individuals but for the development of higher thought processes, both their organization and expression. Certainly Beast retains modern larynx position, so his regression is not complete.

Homo erectus appeared about 1.6 million years ago. These folks were smarter and taller but physically weaker than their forebears were. Beast's head is more like theirs but his body more like that of H. habilus.

Some people still believe that Neanderthals came in between Homo erectus and Homo sapiens. However, a lot of recent evidence contradicts that. For one thing, the Neanderthals were still around about 30,000 years ago, and Homo sapiens proper, our particular Cro-Magnon variety, had developed long before that. So it appears that they were not predecessors to our ancestors, the Cro-Magnons, but contemporaries.

There is some evidence that the Neanderthals were simply Cro-Magnons with dietary deficiencies. If you deprive a modern human of the proper amount of iodine from birth, he or she will grow up looking like a lot like a Neanderthal.

Modern theories now place at least four different kinds of hominids in the same geographical area, in what is now Kenya, over a million years ago. There is evidence that all four groups foraged for food in the same area, but whether or not they interacted, much less interbred, is unknown. What this tells us is that diversity was a keynote of human development, and perhaps, accounts in part for Beast's rather regressive appearance.

Modern humans, Homo sapiens, came along about 100,000 years ago. This date keeps getting pushed back by new discoveries. Only a few years ago, our modern version of human was thought to be only 30-45,000 years old. Like Beast, we have the big head-to-smaller body ratio of our predecessors' children.

METABOLISM

At one point in Beast's career, he injected himself with a formula that, much to his chagrin, devolved him into a brute-like creature that was even hairier and more apish than his usual appearance. Sudden physiological changes are common in regular human-types folk like us, as anyone who has experienced a sudden growth spurt will testify, but not so sudden and not so drastic. We all go through adolescence and its attendant physiological changes. In the adolescent change, hormones inspire the body to increase in size by as much as one third, and this change happens in the span of a few years. To a certain extent, as we gain muscle mass and produce more body hair during this time, we appear to be exhibiting certain "regressive" physical characteristics. (And anyone who has dealt with a growing teenager can testify to the challenge of coping with "regressive" emotional behavior.) Incidentally, overall size change during teenage years is not proportional. The body expands greatly but the head only slightly.

Hormonal changes routinely affect us but non-routine hormone imbalances can mess us up too. Undoubtedly, the ranks of the circus "freaks" who were featured in traveling shows of the nineteenth and early twentieth centuries, the so-called bearded ladies, dog-faced boys, dwarfs, and giants, were all victims of hormonal and developmental imbalances and accidents, not to mention disease. Perhaps a few of them might have been suffering from regressive genetic effects not unlike those that have bedeviled Beast.

PSYCHOLOGICAL EFFECTS

The famous fictional transformation of Dr. Jekyll into the beastly Mr. Hyde in Robert Louis Stevenson's classic tale has a certain resonance with Hank McCoy's saga, and even in the annals of clinical studies of the insane. In certain instances, pathological personality changes can be so severe that the body contorts into a considerably different appearance. Physical strength, too, can be affected, as in the case of mania, when the adrenal glands pump away in support of psychotic fury. But Beast is not mentally afflicted. Nonetheless, it is worthwhile to point out that dramatic psychosomatic changes can be stimulated by one's mental state.

However, such cases all take place over years, not days, as in the case of Beast. This must involve a vastly accelerated metabolic mechanism. Accelerated healing and other metabolic processes have been documented in subjects under the influence of hypnotism and among yogic masters. They are evidently invoking some natural processes, but to this date, no one has been able to isolate any specific hormones to replicate these occurrences. That they are possible is apparent, however.

Beast's poignant dilemma is a favorite fictional device that hearkens back even to the tale of Beauty and the Beast, in which a gentle refined personality resides within the body of a repellent animal. Beast's repellent physical condition may be incurable, but he's got a lot of monstrous company on the bookshelves.

COLOSSUS

Piotr (Peter) Nikolaievitch Rasputin used to work on the Ust-Ordynski Collective farm near Lake Baikal in Siberia with his parents, Nikolai and Alexandra, and his sister and brother, Illyana and Mikhail. Like many mutants, he led a mundane existence until adolescence. Despite the mind-numbing and physically demanding routine of Soviet farm labor, he found an imaginative release in his paintings, for that sturdy, peasant frame contained an artistic soul.

That sturdy frame proved to be quite extraordinary one day. One of the Collective's tractors went out of control and headed toward his sister, Illyana, who was playing nearby, oblivious to her danger. Without hesitation, Piotr rushed to rescue his sister.

The tractor stopped when it struck him while he sustained nary a scratch. In an early demonstration of his power, Piotr had somehow transformed himself into an armored creature with a constitution tough enough to stop a rampaging machine. As with many other X-Men and their mutant adversaries, a personal crisis had activated his latent mutant powers. Not long afterward, Professor Xavier contacted Piotr and asked him to join the X-Men. Difficult though the decision was, Peter took it and began his extraordinary career as an X-Man.

POWERS

Colossus can convert the skin of his entire body into an organic, steel-like substance and he can transform at will virtually instantaneously into this armor-like state. This steel-like substance is of unknown composition but appears to have many of the properties of carbon steel and osmium, a hard blue-white metal in the platinum group that is the hardest known metal. Yet, Colossus' armored skin remains nearly as flexible as normal organic tissue.

While in this state, Colossus possesses the same degree of mobility and agility that he does in his normal form. In fact, when in his armored form, his speed is even somewhat increased, as is his stamina.

He has superhuman strength and a high degree of resistance to bodily harm. His armor is capable of withstanding ballistic penetration, including the impact of a 110 millimeter cannon shell. He could survive a collision with a loaded, one ton flatbed truck at 100 miles per hour or an explosion of 450 pounds of TNT.

He can also survive extremes of temperature from 70° Fahrenheit above absolute zero (about-390° F) to approximately 9,000° F. It is theorized that above this threshold, his armored form would begin to melt. He has little or no need to breathe while in his armored state but it seems unlikely he could survive for long in a vacuum.

Once he converts to his armored form, he remains that way until he consciously wills a conversion to his normal state. But if he is knocked unconscious he immediately returns to his normal form. The longest time he has remained in armored form so far has been five days.

He cannot become partially or selectively armored. It's all or nothing. Even his eyes become steel-like, which doesn't seem to affect his vision and his eyeballs themselves can withstand the impact of gunshots.

When Colossus transforms himself to his armored form he gains additional weight. This might be from an extra-dimensional source. He is in great shape and would get a fine bill of health. This permits the transition back and forth from his normal organic flesh state to his armored form to occur with a minimum of stress on his entire physical system.

CONVERSION OF ELEMENTS

Modern physicists have succeeded in the sort of elemental conversions that the medieval alchemists strove for. (Not, however, the still-elusive "lead-into-gold" maneuver.) One such elemental conversion helped to end World War II: Nuclear bombardment was used to transform uranium into plutonium, which is how one goes about making the basic ingredient for an atomic bomb. But, as atomic reactions have shown, transforming an element isn't so easy. The early experiments in uranium transformation required football field-sized masses of uranium.

Since then, a number of transuranium elements have been created via similar processes: Neptunium, Americium, Curium, Berkelium, Californium, Einsteinium, and several other elements were created this way. The basic concept here involves blasting an element with a bunch of atomic particles until some of them stick and the original element gets heavier. And even if the purpose is only to change the structure of a few atoms, it takes a lot of power to create just a little of a new element.

If Colossus converts himself into something like steel, he must be increasing his weight almost threefold. A lot of mass is coming from somewhere, not to mention the energy needed to perform the conversion.

So elemental conversion is a possibility. But there is a simpler explanation and never go for a complicated one when a simple one will do. (Remember Occam's Razor?)

ORGANIC TRANSFORMATION

As explained in more detail in the entry on Angel, carbon is an extraordinarily flexible and compatible atom that can bond in almost any way a scientist can imagine. Perhaps our good Piotr rearranges the carbon, hydrogen, oxygen, and nitrogen (CHON) atoms of his body into an extremely tough, flexible material.

Teflon and kevlar are synthetic lightweight materials that are, in many respects, tough as steel. They make bulletproof vests out of kevlar and coat bullets with teflon to penetrate them. Teflon, by the way, is made of carbon and fluorine. New carbon compounds are created all the time. And creating new CHON compounds of the sort necessary to make Colossus' skin doesn't require nuclear bombardment. It can only require minimal chemical catalysts.

Although the artificial compounds created so far have been extremely tough, they are not hard. This is another vote in their favor, because Colossus retains his flexibility even when armored. It's entirely reasonable to assume that

Colossus' bodily transformation involves a similar type of compound to these synthetic carbon-based lightweight materials.

HEAT BY-PRODUCTS

As we've suggested elsewhere, some of the super-powered mutants seem to have a body chemistry that produces the equivalent of cold fusion. If that's the case with Colossus, the chemical process must happen very quickly with no evident heat by-product, which would seem unlikely, to put it mildly. Biochemical reactions, both exothermic (the liberation of heat) and endothermic (absorbtion of heat), produce or use a great deal of heat. A more probable hypothesis is that the substance of Colossus' body is composed of exotic tissue that can convert without a biochemical process. It might be a substance that can simply reorganize itself, like water turning to ice. This would not require much energy and could occur very rapidly.

Colossus' flesh is very likely composed of cross-fibered carbon polymers, as we hypothesized with Angel. It would just take a few nerve impulses to cause ligament-like contractions to reorder the layers of striations of his tissues. Even if his tissues were normal flesh, a cross-fibered arrangement would exponentially increase his durability.

This would also explain why concussive blasts don't hurt his internal organs. If he were only covered in a tough armor, his internal organs would still be vulnerable to pressure shocks. But if all his flesh were cross-fibered, it would all be tough, capable of dissipating the force of impact and it wouldn't need to be that hard.

A metal can be very hard and yet still be flexible. In fact, that is why steel is preferred as a construction material over harder alloys and substances. If an extreme force strikes it, steel first bends with the force before breaking. Just as a palm tree can survive a hurricane better than the much harder oak tree, so steel can survive stresses better than harder metals. Similarly, kevlar is more bulletproof than many metals, but not hard at all. It's also worth noting that high grade silk is largely bulletproof. In the old American West, there were reported cases of men shot and killed by bullets that never penetrated their silk bandanas—though the silk did nothing to stop the bullet from entering the wearer's body.

Colossus, when transformed, is certainly no man of steel. He may be a man of kevlar, but it would be a rash person, and its questionable that even Wolverine would dare suggest that he's a man of silk.

ICEMAN

Bobby Drake was the second of the original X-Men. Cyclops recruited him. In the early days he looked more like a snowman than an iceman, and his social affect was juvenile. He was playful and wisecracking. His youthful affect was a helpful and integral part of the team dynamic. He was the one who took the responsibility for lightening the mood when things got tense. This might have been a defense mechanism he'd developed growing up with a father who was rigid, domineering, and inclined to xenophobia reactions. Iceman left the team for a while, becoming first a member of the super hero team called the Champions, then the Defenders, then re-uniting with his original X-Men teammates to form the mutant super group unaffiliated with Professor Xavier known as X-Factor. Finally he, along with the other original X-Men members returned to the X-Men team itself. He has matured quite a bit since his original period with the X-Men, but he never lost his sense of humor.

MOLECULAR MANIPULATION

Iceman can lower his body temperature from the normal 98.6° F to–105.7° F within fractions of a second. His body tissues are seemingly unaffected by subzero temperatures and he retains normal functionality in most respects. There are no known instances of him eating a snack in his frozen state. Perhaps the metabolic processing of normal food is not possible in this state.

As his body temperature falls, the moisture in the air around him condenses and forms a coating of frost and/or ice over his body. When he first completely lowered his body temperature, this covering had a snow-like appearance. As he further lowers his temperature, the covering became crystalline ice. This ice cracks with any movement of his body but new ice constantly replaces it.

In fact, the Iceman has no apparent skeletal structure when he is in his ice-like form. A bullet once went right through him without causing any lasting damage. He has even melted and re-formed. (And without the help of a 12-step program!)

Although he might have started out just coating himself with ice, as his control has increased, he has become able to actually completely transform his bodily structures. Iceman's bodily control now extends to the molecular level.

CREATION OF ICE OBJECTS

Iceman can freeze air moisture into super-hard ice which can then be formed into any object chooses. He is limited only by the amount of moisture available and ambient air temperature, which determines how long his ice sculpture will stay icy. He does not have to hold the ice physically with his hands in order to shape it but can project waves of cold to create ice in the shapes he desires. He has formed ladders, slides, shields, and even bats out of ice.

He can form a column of ice beneath his feet that will raise him off the ground. Its thickness and its steadiness and how well it has been braced determine the strength of the column. A well-braced and regular column, six feet in diameter at its base, is able to support his weight without toppling until it is about 85 feet high and is sturdy enough to endure a 20-mph wind!

He can form long ice-ramps connected either to his ice-column or to existing structures such as buildings and can then travel above the ground by sliding down each ramp as he creates it. However, unless he periodically provides supports, the ramp will crack and break beneath him.

LIMITATIONS

The mental effort needed to employ his mutant power can eventually fatigue him and render his freezing ability temporarily dysfunctional.

His ability to perform is directly related to his physical health and metal state. If he's in decent shape, he can form ice continually for a period of about three hours before becoming fatigued. More trying conditions, such as drawing moisture out of desert air, or healing a hole in his chest, can exhaust him very quickly. Despite being able to control every molecule in his body, he seems to have about normal human strength.

GENETIC ORIGINS

There are animals with unique physiologies that let them function or survive in extreme cold: for example, the birds and fish of the Arctic and Antarctic, and animals such as bears that hibernate in the winter. However, Iceman's power is more exotic. Like the electric eel, he might have a biological mechanism that generates and manipulates energy, in his case producing cold.

TEMPERATURE AND MOLECULAR MOTION

Heat is caused by molecular motion. Cold is the lack thereof. It is quite easy to induce molecular motion and there is some evidence that human race has been doing that since before we could speak. Rub two sticks together, and *voila*, you have molecular motion—heat! Inducing a lack of molecular activity requires something a bit more complex. Technological refrigeration depends on electrically-driven compressors, or pumps, to concentrate some easily compressible medium such as freon or the environmentally-safe compounds, such as the commercial product labeled A-136, that are used today. When A-136 is compressed and pumped through piping and exposed to room temperature, it radiates heat until its molecules slow down and it cools. When the compound is allowed to expand to its normal state, its temperature lowers along with the compound's decompression.

Super-computers, incidentally, use liquid helium, which is more easily compressible, to super-cool their gold-plated circuits. When gold is cooled enough, it becomes a superconductor, which might be Iceman's state to some extent. Keep that in mind as we get to some later ideas.

Iceman obviously does not have an electrically driven compressor, yet he is able to reduce molecular activity.

MAGNETIC COOLING

A newly recognized method of refrigeration is magnetic cooling which was recently used for some landmark experiments. Now, while this is probably not how Iceman works his wintertime magic, it is a very interesting possibility to chew on.

Magnetic cooling takes advantage of the fact that all the atoms in any substance are not all the same temperature. In fact, any substance is composed of a mixture of atoms at various temperatures. We usually measure only the average value.

At the atomic level, temperature translates to energy of atomic motion. High-temperature atoms move more rapidly and forcefully than low-temperature atoms. All atoms can be trapped in a magnetic field, even though not all atoms are naturally magnetic. It just takes a few tricks.

For example, if atoms are given an electrical charge, the movement of the atom with a magnetic field acts like the movement of an electron within the field. This causes a gentle force that can be used to trap the atoms in a specific location.

In the quantum world, nothing can be trapped with absolute certainty. Those atoms with the highest energy—those that move the fastest—will occasionally escape from the magnetic field. Over time, more and more of these high-temperature atoms will escape. Only the low-temperature atoms are left behind. After a few hours of this, the only atoms that remain in the magnetic trap are those with virtually no energy at all—those at or near a temperature of absolute zero. This kind of magnetic cooling device has recently been constructed and has been used to get materials closer to absolute zero than any previous method.

If Iceman were to have a strong internal magnetic field, it is possible that he maintains his low internal temperature by means of magnetic cooling. The higher temperature atoms in his body would, in effect, continually boil off while those that are naturally cool would remain behind. This also provides a potential mechanism to achieve temperatures far below those easily achieved by traditional compressor mechanisms. This also represents a way in which he may keep cool without expending large amounts of energy to do so.

MAXWELL'S DEMON

Magnetic cooling represents an actual, real-world implementation of "Maxwell's Demon." This is an entertaining "thought experiment" that the scientists like to haul out. Physicist James Clerk Maxwell (1831–79) proposed a mechanism of heating and cooling that would require no energy expenditure. He hypothesized a container with a single small hole in its wall. This hole was just big enough to let a single atom or molecule through at one time. Maxwell then imagined a Demon that would sit at the hole watching each atom as it approached from either the inside or the outside of the container. If a cold (low-energy) atom approached from the outside of the container, the Demon would slide open a small gate, allowing the atom to pass through the hole and enter the container. On the other hand, if a high-temperature atom approached from outside the container, the Demon would close the gate, causing the atom to bounce harmlessly off into the environment.

The Demon would use a similar process for atoms approaching the hole from inside the container. A hot atom would be allowed to pass through the hole and exit the container. The relatively cold atom would have the gate closed on it and be trapped within the container. After enough time had passed, the container would be filled with deeply chilled air. Since all the Demon did was open and close a gate, no actual energy to produce heat or cold was expended. Although Maxwell proposed this well before the era of refrigerators, and as a "thought experiment" only, the success of the recent magnetic cooling experiments shows that it works in reality. Perhaps this actually argues for the existence of Maxwell's Demon!

But we are still faced with the problem of where the hot atoms go when Iceman turns on his power. Where is all the heat that boils off? Immense amounts of heat should radiate off of some part of Iceman, such as his back.

EINSTEIN-ROSEN BRIDGES

There is the possibility that the missing heat is simply dumped out of this universe entirely, via micro-wormholes.

This is reminiscent of an analogous procedure utilized by the under-exercised Robert Bruce Banner, Ph.D. in his conversion to the bulked-up Hulk. The extra mass doesn't come from a quick carbo intake and a few steroids shots. It seems to come from another dimension. Perhaps it's another universe entirely rather than just another dimension, for in our universe, the latest theory is that beyond our normal four dimensions, there are another eight or so, all present and accounted for, but curled up in unimaginably small configurations. Wormholes—or Einstein-Rosen bridges as some call them—are a convenient way to get to another universe, and in alternate bubble universes, dimensional configurations could be entirely different.

ENERGY CONVERSION AND DISSIPATION

Another method by which Iceman may dispose of the heat is by converting thermal energy into another form of energy that is more efficiently dissipated. But there are only three other forces and there has been no note of any increase in any of them. (There will be more consideration of the four forces of the universe, shortly.) For the moment let's just say that this method of heat disposal doesn't seem workable.

Both the traditional refrigeration method and magnetic cooling are possibilities might explain Iceman's ability to create cold, but they do not explain his ability to gather moisture out of the air to create ice-objects.

MOLECULAR MANIPULATION

Iceman seems to have a method of controlling the motion of matter. This could be telekinetic control, a power that is shared by a number of other X-Men. By reducing molecular motion directly, he can thereby reduce its temperature. If that is indeed the secret to Iceman's power, direct molecular control would also explain how he is able to gather immense amounts of moisture out of the air to create ice and snow, in various forms.

MAGNETOENCEPHALOGRAPHY

Since all electrical currents generate magnetic fields, the electrical currents caused by the neurons firing in the brain generate minute magnetic fields. A special ultra-sensitive detector known as a SQUID (Super-conducting Quantum Interference Device) can detect these magnetic fields. In this case, super-cooled, super-conducting detectors are able to register the magnetic fields given off by mere thought. This could be a potential mechanism for telekinesis in a super-cooled, and therefore super-conducting, individual.

ELECTRO-MAGNETISM AND THE WEAK FORCE

Another possible way to control molecular activity is manipulation of two of the four physical forces of the universe.

The first two forces of the universe, electromagnetic and gravity, are well known. The second two are a bit more esoteric. They are simply called the strong and weak nuclear binding forces of subatomic matter. You just don't run into those two forces everyday, possibly because they have an effect only at the quantum, or subatomic, level.

What these two do is simply bind subatomic particles together. They are much like gravity, but they work at an infinitesimally smaller level. They are the glue that holds elementary particles, protons and neutrons, together in the core of an atom.

The strong force attracts particles over longer distances and the weak force works only up close. The difference between these two forces is so great that the weak interactive force is weaker by a factor of 10^{12} and might be illustrated as the difference between popping a piece of plastic bubble wrap and an atomic explosion.

But the subatomic world is an area of great differences. The distance between the nucleus of an atom and its first electron shell is like the distance between the Earth and the Sun. If the Sun were the size of a basketball, the Earth would be a peach pit located about a football field's length away. So, broadly speaking, while the weak force works only within the nucleus and the electrons, the strong force works across those large distances.

One of Einstein's greatest projects—and failures—was the attempt to find a Unified Field Theory (see the Magneto entry for more on this) that would explain a relationship between all four forces. But so far, no one has managed to figure out any relationship between electricity and gravity. You can't make something heavier by, say, zapping it with a taser. So there's no proven connection between those two forces. But some work has pointed toward a possible relationship between electromagnetism and the weak force.

This provides us with perhaps the most likely method by which Iceman might have to control molecular activity.

Perhaps through some unusual generation of electric fields, Iceman is able to influence the weak force and rebind matter in new forms, static forms with no molecular motion.

Human beings are known to generate all manner of electrical fields, albeit very weak fields, through neural activity. Some scientists in the former Soviet Union once laid claims to advances in research on the Kirlian fields, the electric field generated by all living things—and even recently deceased things as well. Some aspects of Soviet science, however, were notoriously politicized, and thus suspect in their results. What we'll simply state here is that with regards to experiments on Kirlian fields, Western researchers so far have had a great deal of difficulty duplicating most—but not all—Soviet results in controlled laboratory conditions.

Even though the electrical fields generated by living forms are extremely weak, it might not take much power to effect a great deal of subatomic re-binding. Bear in mind that the colder something is the better it conducts electricity. The less molecular motion there is to impede the flow of current, the more efficiently it moves. This is true for super-conductors in super-computers. It might apply here, as well.

Of course, we are speaking in highly speculative terms, as any relation between the weak binding force and the powers of the electromagnetic spectrum is purely theoretical. However, should we assume that there is such a relation, then we might also assume any number of possibilities of cascading force effects in the quantum (subatomic) world.

Like a chain reaction in a nuclear reactor—where release of the energy of one atom causes the same release in its neighboring atoms—so the increased binding in one subatomic particle might impel similar reactions in nearby particles until an entire molecule stops in motion and in turn halts the motion of surrounding molecules—ultimately resulting in a ski-slope of frozen atmospheric moisture.

This manipulation of the weak force could also be used to gather moisture out of the air. As mentioned earlier, Iceman has created columns of ice 85 feet tall. This would require gathering all the atmospheric moisture for miles around. It leads one to theorize that if his water-gathering powers are so strong, they would be at their most formidable at sea. Were he to encounter Magneto on, say Tahiti, he might be able to belt him with a glacier or two.

Whether Iceman freezes through telekinetic manipulation of matter or through electromagnetic influence on the weak binding force of subatomic matter, we remain faced with the separate question of how he can survive. Frogs frozen in pond mud have been known to revive with the spring thaw and experiments in the cryogenic area have induced such hibernation states in more complicated organisms such as lab mice; and there are the examples of bears and other mammals that hibernate during the winter. The main problem with actually freezing a living creature is that, if not properly controlled, ice crystals form and rupture cell membranes. The brain is particularly susceptible to freezing damage. Also, with respect to freezing and cryogenics, the result makes the organism totally immobile. Iceman, in contrast, not only survives freezing intact, but also continues to function even with a body temperature as low as—107°F. This returns us to the concept of molecular control, whether through telekinesis or weak force manipulation.

There is a third possibility. Perhaps he can move by some molecular analog of superconductivity. When the temperature of certain materials is lowered to close to absolute zero, the resistance to electrical current flowing through them becomes very small. Perhaps his molecules generate no friction and can slide over each other with ease, enabling him to move by rolling over himself, as it were.

SUPER-COOLING

Since super-cooled matter conducts electricity with no resistance, intense electrical currents can be carried without generation of heat. If such intense currents were to flow in his body, they would generate equally intense magnetic fields. These magnetic fields would maintain the magnetic cooling effect discussed earlier and so maintain his temperature. They would also exert physical forces on any other matter that happened to be carrying a strong electrical current, such as Iceman's own body. This may be the secret of his ability to occasionally change shape. If this were the case, it would be prudent for him not to carry credit cards, as he would erase the magnetic strip on each one.

There is a precedent for unusual molecular activity in super cooled substances. Helium, if cooled to nearly absolute zero, assumes some strange properties. One form of super-cooled helium will actually crawl uphill and literally climb out of bottles thanks to the power of surface tension and, perhaps, the strong and weak binding forces. In any case, the strong and weak forces become much more important at very low temperatures, so therefore might be an explanation of Iceman's powers.

STRENGTH AND SPEED

If Iceman is able to make his frozen body bend and move as fast as normal human flesh and to lift and jump and punch with the usual amount of human strength, what limits his speed and strength?

BOSE-EINSTEIN CONDENSATE

Here's one last possibility to consider: Some recently-performed experiments may provide important insights into Iceman's physiology.

Years ago, Albert Einstein predicted that if a collection of atoms were cooled sufficiently, the atomic nuclei would emerge and form a single super-atom that is now known as a Bose-Einstein condensate. Until recently, this was only hypothetical. However, a few months ago, a group of scientists used magnetic cooling and some other tricks to cause a group of metal atoms to merge into a true Bose-Einstein condensate.

This first condensate consisted of only about 30 or so atoms. Subsequently, this group and several others have made condensates consisting of up to 1,000 component atoms. A Bose-Einstein condensate is considered to be a completely new form of matter. Since the atoms in it lose their individual identity, the mechanical and chemical properties of a Bose-Einstein condensate are completely unknown. What is known is that the Bose-Einstein condensate is a natural super-conductor. It is felt likely that there is no friction between the original components whatsoever.

Given the different properties and abilities Iceman has exhibited, it is tempting to say, "Eureka! Iceman is one large Bose-Einstein condensate!" because that would neatly explain how he can do what he does. But science trains us to conduct a thorough examination, we'll simply have to leave it as an hypothesis. Even so, it's nice to have Einstein in one's court—even at the hypothetical level.

ROGUE

Rogue, whose real name has never been revealed, can absorb the memories, feelings, abilities, physical characteristics, skills, knowledge, languages, fighting styles and even mystic arts of anyone—mutant or non—with whom she comes into flesh-to-flesh contact. Like Cyclops with his optic force beams, her power is permanently stuck in the "on" position. And like Cyclops, she uses aids to prevent accidental use of her power; in her case, she wears gloves and makes sure that her body is covered as completely as possible.

Rogue has additional powers, including invulnerability, super strength, flight and a precognitive "seventh" sense that enables her to anticipate an enemy's action during the course of battle. Most of these were permanently absorbed from the Super Hero Ms. Marvel. We'll be focusing on rogue's natural mutant ability, her absorbtion power.

Her skin must directly contact the skin of her subject in order for the absorption to take place. She cannot absorb by touch if she wears gloves, nor if she touches her subject through their clothing.

Her absorption powers are ineffective against artificial life forms (robots), pure energy beings, non-sentient life forms (lower orders of animals and all plants), and dead or inorganic objects.

The transfer of abilities and memories works on about a 1:60 ratio. One second of contact transfers the victim's abilities and memories to Rogue for 60 seconds. One minute of contact translates into an hour's transfer. If Rogue maintains the contact for too long, as she did with Ms. Marvel, she will permanently absorb the other person's powers and memories. The consequences of such prolonged contact are severe; Ms. Marvel almost died and Rogue almost went insane. Neither has fully recovered from the contact, and each suffers from occasional recidivism.

PARASITES

Parasites survive by taking something they need from their host. In nature parasites absorb nutrition, usually blood, from the host organism. Parasites range from e. coli, tuberculosis and HIV, to tapeworms, mosquitos and leeches and moray eels, lampreys vampire bats. Parasites may have one or multiple hosts, and often cannot survive outside of them. The type of "nutrition" that Rogue steals from her hosts is mental and/or psychic. Her ability calls to mind the belief of many primitive Neolithic cultures—that if you eat your enemy you will absorb their prowess.

Although Rogue's parasitic effects vary, her short-term contact victims seem to recover entirely. In the case of these temporary transfers, Rogue's subjects lose their abilities for exactly the amount of time that Rogue takes them on. When she effects the transfer, the victim loses consciousness and will ordinarily remain unconscious until the transfer wears off. If a victim is awakened before the transfer ends, the victim's mind will be vacant. However, the victim suffers no permanent injury.

LIFE FORCE

At first blush, life force sounds like a mystical concept of the soul, an essence of being that exists independently of the body. However, when we break it down, we find something far more mundane.

We are mostly water—about 60 percent. The remaining 40 percent is primarily CHON (carbon, hydrogen, oxygen, and nitrogen). That's mostly gas and there are trace elements of heavier stuff and a noticeable amount of calcium in the skeletal structure.

Where exactly does a "life force" fit in this? Obviously, we're not just talking about the electrical fields attendant to cerebral and other metabolic processes. If that were the case, Rogue could just pocket a couple of D-size alkaline batteries at any corner store. And she certainly doesn't use the matter of a body itself, or a supermarket steak would fill the bill.

It's not just any old CHON that works for her. It's got to be living matter. She can't drain matter out of a chair. And, it seems animals won't do the trick either. Only human life force will give her a large charge.

We like to use the logical tool of Occam's Razor whenever possible and keep things simple as possible. Never use two explanations when one will do. However, there's just no single physical reason why she can't have a chimp for a snack instead of a certified public accountant. There's got to be a psychological, not physical, reason why she "eats" people instead of animals. There's really nothing in living matter that she can't find in inanimate, inorganic materials. However, she might need a living human mind to help her do her dirty work.

PSIONIC RESONANCE

Professor X can't make telepathic contact with animals. Perhaps he requires a human brain to be "in sync" for telepathic communication. Similarly, Rogue might need that sort of syncing-up to enable her power to take effect. A psionic resonance—like-mind to like-mind—might be the prerequisite for her powers to work. Perhaps she needs her subject's brain to complete a circuit and create a feedback-like amplification effect to reach the critical levels necessary to activate the process.

Just as the psionic powers of other X-Men can be used as telekineticism to manipulate matter, so too might Rogue use her psionic powers to "lockstep" the matter of her own body with that of her subject. If she is using the mind of her subject as a psionic resonator, the process might well leave the subject a bit rattled. This would account for amnesia and other symptoms of psychic shock.

Rogue's parasitic ability is far more sophisticated than what exists in the lower orders, but it has the same ultimate object—her safety and survival.

TECHNOLOGY

Professor X has enough Ph.D.s to fill a house with inventions . . . and he has. The Xavier Mansion houses the psionic-detecting machine, Cerebro and the Danger Room, which is filled with fantastic training devices. On the grounds of the Mansion stands the air hangar for the Blackbird jet. All of these are integrated with the advanced technology of the alien Shi'ar race.

The enemies of the X-Men have advanced technology of their own to draw upon. The robotic mutant-hunting Sentinels have been upgraded by a series of designers over the years and it looks like this will go on for some time, as even more advanced models from alternate futures keep coming back through time to pursue the mutants.

Development of the technology of most of human history depended upon advances in materials. Over the course of 100,000 years, we had two Stone Ages (the Paleolithic and the Neolithic), the Copper Age, the Bronze Age and then the Iron Age. In the past two centuries, we had revolutions in power, as we progressed from steam to electricity to nuclear power. During the past half century, we had the upheaval of communications technology. Judging from the applications we have seen of Shi'ar and future technologies, perhaps the next stage of scientific and technological development will once again be in the areas of power and materials. The future tech seems capable of fantastic power—enough to propel a starship to light speed—and of astonishingly tough materials: robots that can withstand powerful blasts and starships that can withstand the rigors of trans-Einsteinian speeds.

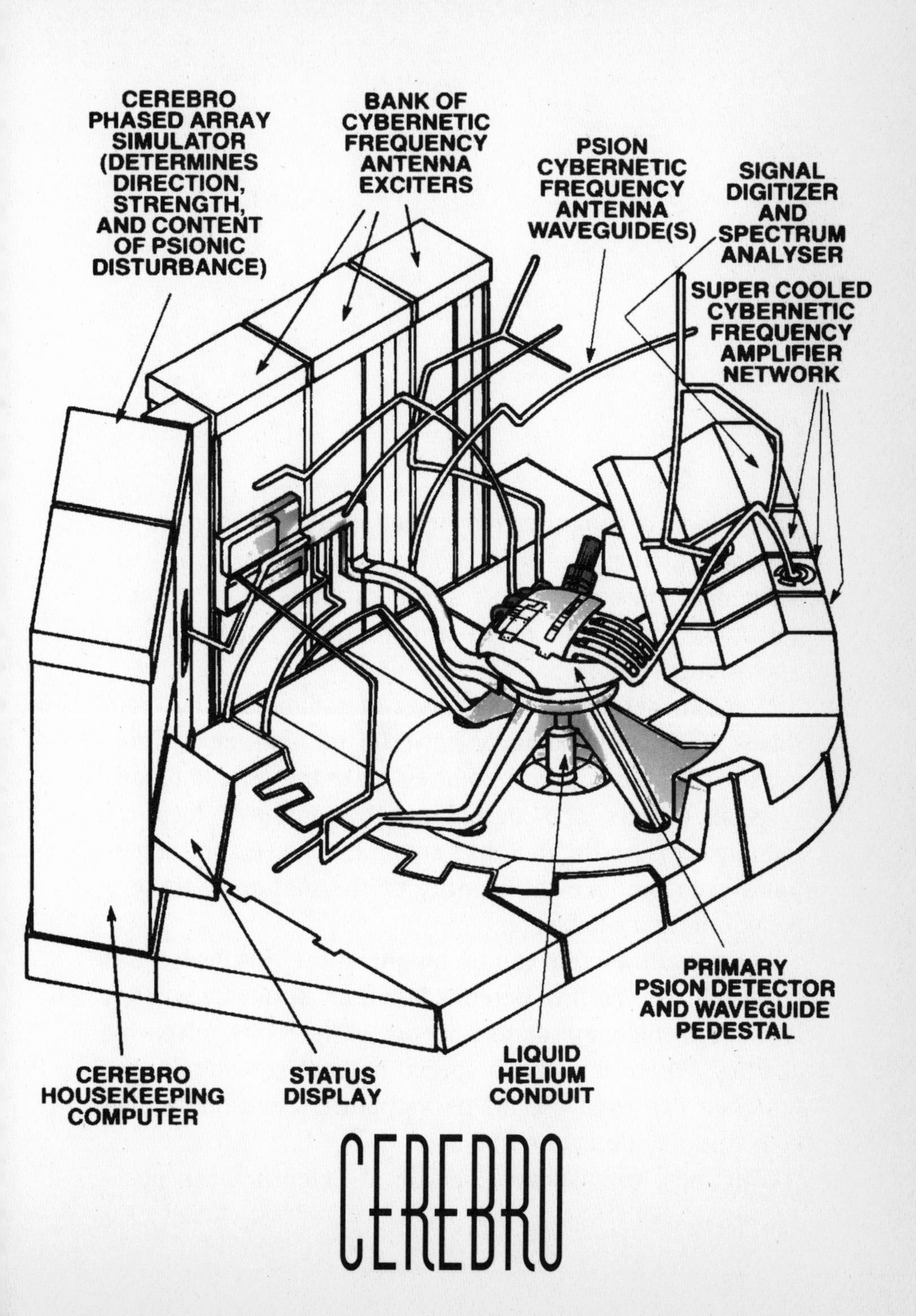
CEREBRO PHASED ARRAY SIMULATOR (DETERMINES DIRECTION, STRENGTH, AND CONTENT OF PSIONIC DISTURBANCE)
BANK OF CYBERNETIC FREQUENCY ANTENNA EXCITERS
PSION CYBERNETIC FREQUENCY ANTENNA WAVEGUIDE(S)
SIGNAL DIGITIZER AND SPECTRUM ANALYSER
SUPER COOLED CYBERNETIC FREQUENCY AMPLIFIER NETWORK
PRIMARY PSION DETECTOR AND WAVEGUIDE PEDESTAL
CEREBRO HOUSEKEEPING COMPUTER
STATUS DISPLAY
LIQUID HELIUM CONDUIT

CEREBRO

Cerebro is a computerized detection device designed by Professor Charles Xavier to find mutant humans with superhuman abilities. In this respect, its intended function is not unlike that of the much-feared mutant-detecting Sentinel robots.

Cerebro detects distinct waves of psionic energy-brain waves which superhumanly powerful mutants emit. Cerebro's software can process and evaluate the psionic broadcasts it detects and determine the mutant's location, roughly measure the mutant's amount of power, and sometimes even produce the identity of the mutant if there is enough data available.

Just about anyone can be taught to use this device, but Professor X is the pro. Cerebro functions optimally when it is linked to his mind or to someone with similar telepathic abilities. When he wears a special headset connection, the Professor can even use his psionic powers to amplify Cerebro's psionic detection ability.

The most sophisticated version of Cerebro, when operated by its most sophisticated user, Professor X, can search hundreds, if not thousands, of miles. On occasion, it has detected mutants on distant continents. However, at the farther reaches of its detection range, it seems to become less specific in pinpointing locations. That's when the field team is sent in to do the search.

X-Men have sometimes carried smaller versions of the device, "portable Cerebros," with them. A portable Cerebro is in telemetric contact with the main computer console and can detect the presence of mutants at short range.

Xavier began development of Cerebro before he founded the X-Men. He used an early version of the device, which he called Cyberno, to locate Scott Summers, who was Xavier's first recruit for the X-Men (see the Cyclops entry). Xavier completed the first true Cerebro machine shortly after Jean Grey joined the team.

Cerebro was named after the human cerebrum, the largest and most recently evolved part of the human brain. This is also the part of the brain responsible for the transmission of psionic waves.

ARTIFICIAL INTELLIGENCE

Cerebro has varying degrees of artificial intelligence and can detect psionic waves. (For more on psionic powers, see the entries for Jean Grey, Mastermind, and Professor X. For more on some actual physical senses that all of us have that are sometimes confused with psionic senses, see the entry for Wolverine.)

Artificial Intelligence (AI) was first defined by British scientist Alan Turing (1912–1954), who devised a test for artificial intelligence known as, naturally, the Turing Test. The Turing Test for AI required that a human being converse with a disembodied voice coming through a speaker for five minutes without being able to discern whether the voice belonged to a human or a machine. (A joke that made the rounds at Massachusetts Institute of Technology a few years ago was that the undergraduate students had such underdeveloped social skills that they couldn't pass for human in any conversation, and several undergrads proudly wore T-shirts that read, "I flunked the Turing Test.")

One of the first attempts to pass the Turing test was a program called Eliza. You would type in a question such as, "How are you today, Eliza?" and the program would respond, "How do you think I am? Why are you so concerned about me?" (Some of you might have had boy or girlfriends who might have flunked the Turing test.) But it does mean that intelligence is very complicated. So let's make a distinction between computer intelligence and higher intelligence.

The number of possible neuron connections in the human brain far exceeds the estimated number of electrons in the universe. That doesn't mean that all such neuron connections result in rational thought, but intelligence is not always rational (as anyone acquainted with other human beings knows). It does mean that intelligence is very complicated.

As F. David Peat notes the distinction between intelligence and intellect in "Artificial Intelligence: How Machines Think,": "Intellect could be thought of as the more fixed aspects of intelligence. Intelligence, however, has the capacity for constant creativity, the emergence of novelty, and of concepts and structures that are in a continual state of flux.

"It does indeed seem possible that with sufficient hard work, the human intelligence will eventually be able to reproduce the achievements of its intellect within electronic machines. However, the possibility of developing true intelligence—an infinite creative capacity of change—seems remote."

A favorite theme of science fiction literature and film is one in which super-intelligent computers dominate—and subjugate—less capable human beings. Frankly, the cheap thrills and fear that this sort of premise generates is not only foolish, but counterproductive.

It's the assumption of many scientists that eventually computers will be designed that will be able to learn on their own, accumulating and sorting new information and developing new and possibly ever-more-sophisticated means of solving problems.

NANOTECHNOLOGY

One field of "computer intelligence" that is currently being explored falls in the realm of medical technology: scientists are working on developing tiny intelligent machines that could travel within the human body to diagnose and/or repair tissue damage. Such nanotechnology, if fully developed, would certainly be a benign and desirable example of artificial intelligence.

Another intriguing possibility is that future developments in computers will involve building computers out of living tissue. In this case, such bio-computers would surely be able to interact with human bodies—and brains—in surprising ways, perhaps even creating a bio-cybernetic linkage between human brain and machine computer that might qualify as yet another form of intelligence.

SENTINELS

The Sentinels are giant robots that were designed to locate and either capture or kill superhuman mutants. Usually the Sentinels are controlled by a Master Mold, a leader or "prime unit" among the robots that functions as a director for all drone activities. There have been several different models of the Sentinels. They are all equipped with mutant-tracking sensors, lasers, catchwebs, disintegrator beams and other weapons.

MARK I

Dr. Bolivar Trask designed the first Sentinels and hired a large team of cyberneticists, roboticists, and engineers to construct them. They were programmed to protect humanity from mutants, but their cybernetic logic led them to the conclusion that they should take control of human society. Consequently, the Sentinels turned on Dr. Trask, captured him and forced him to make them even more powerful. Filled with remorse over the "Frankenstein monsters" he had created, Dr. Trask attempted to destroy them. He succeeded in destroying the first Master Mold at the cost of his life. Unfortunately, that proved not to be the end of the Sentinels.

Mark I Sentinels had great strength and flew with high efficiency turbine jets in their feet. They had various weapons, such as electron beams, plasma blasters, and lasers in their chests or hands, depending on the model. They had an communications and navigation equipment in their heads, an all-band spectrum analyzer in their chests, a CPU in their bellies—a safe and sensible location, unlike ours. They were covered with flexible micro chainmail armor.

MARK II

The Mark II was developed by Lawrence "Larry" Trask after his father's death. Some Mark IIs, such as the leader, were built from the leftovers of the originals, but many new ones were built from scratch.

Various weapons systems were added to the Mark II. Their computer systems were more sophisticated than the first versions. Like the originals, they had great strength and could fly via jet propulsion units in their feet. They could also project strong steel tendrils, powerful force blasts, and jets of knockout gas or steam from their palms.

MARK III

Dr. Steven Lang got access to the plans for the Sentinels and constructed the Mark III. This was inferior to the earlier models. The notes Lang worked from were incomplete and the secrecy of his activities prevented him from employing as many specialists as the Trasks had. As well, to make sure that these Sentinels could never turn against him, Lang made them less intelligent than their predecessors.

The Mark III series were built in the form of the original X-Men. Nevertheless, the X-Men destroyed them. Lang was left in a brain-dead coma but his brain engrams were imprinted in the computer-brain of his own 30-foot tall Master Mold. This was later destroyed in an encounter with the Hulk.

MARKS IV AND V

Sebastian Shaw, evil mutant and leader of the secret and sinister Hellfire Club whose goal is to covertly control the world's governments, produced two models of Sentinels, Mark IV and Mark V. Neither of these is as dangerous as the Mark II series.

Mark IV Sentinels stood 20 feet tall and could release steel tendrils from their hands. Mark V Sentinels were also 20 feet tall and could fly with jet propulsion units in their feet, release energy blasts and sleep gas blasts from their hands, and project beams of intense cold from their eyes. They are equipped with sensors that could analyze both human and mutant opponents.

ALTERNATE SENTINELS

There are also two models of Sentinels that were created in the future of an alternate Earth. The Omega series Sentinels have tremendous strength, high resistance to damage, and propulsion units in their feet. Like Mark II Sentinels they could analyze an opponent's abilities and adjust their weapons systems to deal with his or her powers. Like the Mark

III, they could fire energy blasts from their palms and fire non-metallic "catchwebs" from their fingers in order to imprison opponents. They have self-repair systems.

The most deadly Sentinel of all, the Nimrod, traveled to the X-Men's history-line and hunted mutants. Among its many weapons were tight-beam high-frequency sound waves and a synapse-dislocater that jams neural impulses.

The Sentinels keep getting deadlier but the X-Men keeping gaining in experience. It seems the human learning curve still slopes up faster than the Sentinels' cybernetic adaptations systems can follow.

ARTIFICIAL INTELLIGENCE

The giant Sentinels are capable of adapting, learning and modifying themselves after each encounter with mutants. Regardless of their model number, what the Sentinels share is Artificial Intelligence (AI). AI was first defined by British scientist Alan Turing, who devised a test for artificial intelligence known as, naturally, the Turing Test. Basically, the Turing Test is as follows, if a person is having a conversation with a subject that s/he cannot see, and cannot tell from the answers whether or not the subject is human or a computer, then de facto the computer is displaying artificial intelligence. Presently, no known commercially available computer is capable of displaying AI. If the government has one, it's not talking—or, maybe it is and we can't tell.

As computers become steadily, exponentially more sophisticated and capable, perhaps one day AI will be the outcome of computer development, and computers will not only design themselves but upgrade themselves in much the same fashion as the Sentinels.

PARTICLE AND OTHER BEAMS

All the Sentinels have some form of power beams. Their technology is obviously greatly advanced over ours, but we have managed to make some power beams of our own. Let's look at different commercially available beams and see how they compare to those of the Sentinels.

Particle beams come in two flavors: charged electrons or protons and neutral neutrons or hydrogen atoms.

You might not realize it but you probably have the first kind of particle beam already, and you use it every day in the privacy of your own home. PC monitors and televisions have cathode ray tubes with electron beams. These are particle beam accelerators: a heated filament makes electrons, high voltage plates accelerate them, and electric and magnetic fields focus them into a beam that strikes the surface of the television screen.

In theory, particle beams are marvelously powerful, but in reality there's the problem of power, focus and control, propagation, equipment size, and expense. It's a bummer, but the fact is that to make a particle beam as powerful as the beams the Sentinels use would require particles accelerated to the order of one thousand million electron volts at currents of 1,000 amps sustained for 0.1 of a millisecond. That's a million megawatts of power, which is far above anything possible in our technology.

What's more, the beam spreads out as it travels because of the repulsion between particles with the same charge. A one-inch wide electron beam will spread out to about 45 feet by the time it gets less than 1,000 miles away. A similar proton beam would spread to almost 18 miles in width. And that's in a completely clear vacuum without any magnetic or gravity fields to get in the way.

Now, whenever the Sentinels use their beams, it's usually at pretty close range—under a thousand yards. But any dispersion weakens the impact of the beam. The more focused it is, the more power is needed. Power is a real problem: these beams need a lot of it.

Neutron particle beams wouldn't spread out as much because the particles all have the same charges and don't repel each other. But the particles must start with an electrical charge so they could be accelerated and focused. Then the beam would have to be neutralized, which would make it spread. Hardly worth the effort.

One way to lower the dispersion rates for all three types of beams would be to burn a vacuum tunnel through the air with a high power laser before firing the particle beam. But why go to the trouble? If we could make a high power laser that would burn such a tunnel, why not use that as a weapon by itself? In that case, who needs a particle beam?

Although the propagation problems aren't too daunting in outer space, the huge size of the accelerators required, and the great power demands as well as the need for precise control in an extremely variable magnetic environment, makes the development of a space-based particle beam weapon look mighty unlikely.

Serious particle accelerators, like the ones used in scientific research could reach extremely high energy levels. The huge Fermi accelerator, say, could accelerate protons to 500 thousand million electron volts. Fusion reactors could make particle beams at much lower energies.

But the Sentinels aren't carrying mile-long particle accelerators in their pockets.

The way things stand now; particle beams don't seem particularly useful as weapons. They could indeed make for some pretty deadly firepower, but would be a lot more expensive than many weapons we already have. Even if we did use such high-tech deadly toys, there are a lot of cheap counter measures which could be used to dissipate the beam before it ever hits the target, or reduce the effect if it does manage to hit. A cloud of dust in the air is all it would take to make the beam widen and weaken.

LASERS

LASER is an acronym or abbreviation of the first letters of Light Amplification through Stimulated Emission of Radiation. A laser is a very thin glass tube, about the size of a drinking straw, containing a gas. Most of the lasers used to make holograms use helium and neon. Electricity passes through this gas and it glows. There are two mirrors at the ends of the tube Light bounces back and forth between them. One of the mirrors is completely silvered and is completely reflective. The other mirror is only partially silvered and lets some of the light pass through it, resulting in your basic laser beam. The mirrors essentially produce a feedback cycle of light, building up the power and focussing its frequency.

Lasers don't have the dispersion problems of particle beams and therefore might be a weapon of choice for the Sentinels. What's more, it's possible to get enough energy into a short-range laser beam to destroy a target under good atmospheric conditions. However, any dust, smoke, clouds, or opaque and/or reflective solids in the beam's path will block and weaken the laser radiation. Future development of lasers will probably yield much better—i.e. more destructive—results.

The most exotic lasers are chemical, free electron and

X-ray lasers. They have higher power and higher frequencies. Higher frequencies transmit farther so that's a great advantage.

Chemical lasers use hydrogen or deuterium and fluorine as fuels and reach outputs greater than one megawatt. Not bad, but still not high enough to match the Sentinels' beams. Excimer krypton-fluoride lasers are higher frequency but are far lower in power. Free electron lasers are adjustable so that the best frequency could be chosen, but the higher the power is raised, the lower frequencies fall. X-ray laser beams could be produced with a nuclear explosion as the energy source. This really isn't very practical. Leaving aside the most obvious problem, you'd get only one beam blast out of each nuke and it would be mighty hard to aim it.

As we've stated above, the laser doesn't have the dispersion problems that particle beams have and it's possible to get enough energy into a short-range laser beam to destroy a target in good atmospheric conditions. However, the laser would have to be held on the target for awhile to burn through. They don't cut through steel like a hot knife through butter, more like a hair dryer melting through a block of ice. And, as we know, any dust, smoke, clouds, or anything opaque or reflective to light will block and weaken the laser radiation.

Future development of lasers have the potential to yield better results. One possibility could be a ground-based laser site focused on a space mirror. That could solve the problems of weight, size of power supplies, and fuel requirements. Of course, you wouldn't be able to carry it around with you, but a communications link could guide targeting. Potentially, you could zap anything, anywhere beneath the footprint of the space mirror.

JET PROPULSION

The Sentinels have rockets in their feet that let them fly. These foot-jets must be radically different from any jet known to us as they seem to operate without air intake. If a jet engine doesn't take in air, it has nothing to jet out. Propulsion is generally accomplished by propelling something in the opposite direction from where you are heading. Jet engines do this by explosively burning high octane, ultra-refined petroleum-based fuels so that they blow air out of their rear exhausts. The air gets super-heated by the explosive burning fuel. However, just producing a lot of heat won't propel you through the air. But a ready source of heat energy will drive air ahead of it at a good speed. Nuclear explosions drive shock waves through the air at supersonic velocities. Whatever the Sentinels' energy source, it must do something similar. Let's take a close look at real jets and rockets and see how they work.

THE PRINCIPLE OF JET PROPULSION

We're back to Sir Isaac Newton here. That clever guy actually built a jet wagon. Newton's Third Law of Motion states that for every action there is an equal and opposite reaction. He tested it by creating a water-filled sphere that was heated by fire, creating steam. A large nozzle projected back from the sphere. A jet of steam shot out of the nozzle. That was the action and the forward movement of the wagon was the reaction. The same principle applies to jet engines, and for this reason they are called reaction engines.

If you open the neck of a blown-up balloon, it zips off. It is not the air rushing out of the neck and pushing against the outside air that drives the balloon ahead but the air pushing against the inside front wall of the balloon that actually propels it. A jet engine would work even better in a vacuum because there would be no air resistance to slow down the jetting gases.

BREATHING AND BREATHLESS JET ENGINES

There are two general types of jet propulsion: Non-air-breathing engines and air breathing. Air-breathing engines use oxygen from the atmosphere in the combustion of fuel. They fall into two categories: those with compressors and those without.

Turbojets and turboprops have compressors, usually turbine-driven, to take in air. They are called gas-turbine engines. The turbojet is the most widely used air-breathing engine. With turbojets, air is drawn into the engine and a compressor increases its pressure. The air enters a combustion chamber where it is mixed with a finely atomized kerosene-like fuel and burned. The heat makes it expand and drives it through a wheel-like device called a turbine, which it turns, producing power. The hot air goes out through an exhaust nozzle, which squeezes and increases its speed. It is that final high-velocity jet that produces the thrust to push the plane through the air.

Turboprops, or propjets, are hybrid jets and propeller planes that have turbine driven compressors and propellers. This creates some thrust from the jets but produces most of it from the propellers. Afterburners are added to turbojets to increase thrust. They are auxiliary combustion chambers, attached to the tail pipe, in which additional fuel is burned to utilize unused oxygen in the exhaust gases from the turbine.

Unlike turbojets and turboprops, pulsejets and ramjets

do not have compressors. The noisy pulsejet engine powered the German V-1 buzz bomb during World War II. Pulsejets have to be boosted to high speed by some other kind of propulsion to start combustion. Buzz bombs were basically fired like cannon shells to get them going. Ramjets have to be kick-started this way too.

Pulsejets are noisy because they are intermittent-firing jets. At the front end of pulsejets, shutters intermittently open and close to take in air. This creates a series of rapid explosions. They are not as efficient as turbojets or ramjets.

Ramjets are the simplest jet engines because they have no moving parts. They are fire continuously and are open-ended smoke pipes that ram air in as the engines move forward and burn fuel continuously to produce forward thrust. They are used for missiles and experimental aircraft.

Non-air-breathing engines, or rockets, carry an oxygen supply. These can be used both in the atmosphere and in space. The World War II German V-2 missile was powered by a rocket engine. Rocket engines are also used in research planes and missiles. The Sentinels must use non-breathing jets, as they are capable of space travel.

There are three kinds of rockets-liquid-propellant, solid propellant, and the most innovative of all, the electric engines. Spaceships on deep-space missions, such as the Voyager, use electric engines. These engines produce low thrust for long periods. There are three types: arc-jets, ion/electrostatics, and plasma/magnetohydrodynamics.

The arc-jet, or electrothermal, engine utilizes an electric arc discharge to heat a propellant gas. The gas expands through a nozzle, producing thrust. The ion, or electrostatic, engine employs cesium ions accelerated by an electrostatic field to create thrust. The plasma, or magnetohydrodynamic

(MHD), engine uses an ionized gas accelerated by an electromagnetic field to produce thrust.

WEAPONS FLEXIBILITY AND ADAPTABILITY

The Sentinels weapons systems are remarkably responsive and adaptive. But perhaps that's not so far off in our own technology. Consider the feedback mechanism already at work in our own automobiles' cruise controls. At the press of a button, voila, the car maintains a steady speed selected by the driver. This is achieved by a sensor that measures the car's speeed, controlling the carburetor and boosting the fuel flow if the car's speed begins to drop for any reason. If, for example, the car is moving uphill and needs more fuel to maintain the required speed, the sensor measures this and provides additional fuel. Or if the car is moving downhill and exceeding the set speed, the sensor can feed less fuel to the engine.

The sensor may be an electromagnet on the drive shaft, which would produce an electric signal related to the car's speed. A microprocessor could continually check out the sensor signal and relay control signals to the motor. Further, a microprocessor could not only control speed but calculate and display speed, distance, and fuel consumption, controlling the engine to affect the latter.

Obviously, the Sentinels' nanotechnology has not only solved but refined this process, taking this principle to the "X-degree."

XAVIER MANSION

The headquarters for the X-Men and related groups is the Xavier Mansion at 1407 Graymalkin Lane in the town of Salem Center in New York State's Westchester Country. The Xavier estate stretches over a broad area between Graymalkin Lane and Breakstone Lake.

The mansion belongs to the founder of the mutant teams, Profes-sor Charles Xavier. Ten generations ago, the mansion was built by a Dutch seafarer named Xavier. It was constructed from local stone quarried at the edge of Breakstone Lake.

Over the past two centuries, the mansion has been renovated, electrified, given indoor plumbing, and otherwise modernized. In the latter half of this century, facilities were installed and constructed for use by the X-Men.

The mansion was actually destroyed once but was rebuilt with the incorporation of advanced alien Shi'ar technology (see entry on Shi'ar). It now functions in as a sophisticated fortress for the X-Men and other mutant teams.

The mansion is publicly known as a respected private school with a highly limited enrollment. Originally named Professor Xavier's School for Gifted Youngsters, it is now the Xavier Institute for Higher Learning. That the mansion also serves as the headquarters of the X-Men is a carefully-kept secret. Of course, the school's students are actually covert team members of the X-Men and other mutant teams.

Let's work our way up from the bottom, shall we?

SUBBASEMENT Level One

The subbasements were constructed only in recent years. Level One, is primarily given over to extensive medical facilities. These include an extensively equipped operating theatre and a large recovery room that can easily hold 25 patient beds.

There is also an Olympic-size swimming pool-for indoor use when it is too cold to use the outdoor pool. As well, there are a sauna, steam bath, a fully equipped gymnasium, and locker rooms, not to mention various laboratory facilities and the terminal for the high speed magnetic rail cars that are used to reach the aircraft hangars through the adjoining underground tunnel.

MAGNETIC LEVITATION TRAIN

The high speed magnetic rail cars that run from Level One of the sub-basement of the Xavier Mansion to the aircraft hangars are probably magnetic levitation, or "maglev" trains. A maglev train has no wheels. It levitates above a track called a guideway and is pro-pelled by magnetic fields.

When the train is moving it is suspended in the air above

the tracks by magnetic repulsion. When it stops, it is docked by magnetic attraction.

Alternating magnetic repulsion and attraction propel the train along its track. A series of powerful electromagnets located along the guide rail create a moving magnetic wave. The maglev train is carried by this wave in the same manner as a surfer is carried by a wave in the ocean.

DANGER ROOM

In the Level Two of the sub-basement of the Xavier Mansion is the new, improved Danger Room. Most of the new Shi'ar technology that the X-Men have acquired is installed on this level.

The original Danger Room, where Xavier trained mutants in the use of their powers, was on the mansion's first floor and employed the most advanced technology available at the time. (That even included robots!)

The new Danger Room uses extraterrestrial Shi'ar technology, which includes extraordinarily advanced holographic projectors. Almost any environment can be simulated here, which comes in handy for training mutants in how to deal with a variety of threatening opponents without much actual wear and tear on the mutants. There are also alternate living quarters here and other backup facilities.

HOLOGRAPHIC TECHNOLOGY

There are many unusual and fascinating features to the Danger Room but the main one we want to focus on is the holographic equipment. It is far more sophisticated than any contemporary holographic technology. In order to understand the basis of the Shi'ar holographs, let's look at what Earth science has been able to develop.

A hologram is more or less just normal photographic film but it has been exposed to a laser, which captures light wave interference patterns, rather than to normal light. This results in three-dimensional images.

Because the viewed 3-D image appears to float in front of the film, people often think that holograms can somehow be projected into thin air. However, the viewer must always be looking at or through the hologram. Viewing angles are usually limited to one or two people at a time, and image size is usually one cubic meter or less.

At present, there are no free-floating holograms. Future developments might give us larger film sizes or even moving 3-D holograms, but present technology gives us nothing remotely approaching that, let alone free-floating images.

There *are* a variety of types of 3-D processes for film and video but all have very limited depth and are not true holograms. Besides, they require special glasses to be seen. Most 3-D film uses only two images, one for each eye. The 3-D effect is dependent on techniques such as light polarization, gray scale changes, red and green images, or separate video feeds for each eye.

So, holograms are not projected. Rather, light fills up a hologram film like gelatin would fill up a mold. In a technical sense, holograms are reconstructions of the light that reflected off the object. An image composed of nothing but light, even coherent laser-like light, cannot just float freely in space. Light is always on the move, traveling constantly and consistently at about 186,000 miles per second.

HOLOGRAM OR HOLOGRAPH?

There is some confusion as to whether the correct word is hologram or holograph. Let's clear that up. The best word is hologram. A holographer is someone who makes holograms. Holography is the word for the technology and artform of the hologram. Things that relate to holography are holographic. But the thing itself is not a holograph. It is a hologram. Make sense?

The first three-dimensional holographic images were created by University of Michigan researchers Leith and Juris Upatnieks in the early 60s. Around this time, Yuri Dennisyuk of the former Soviet Union also began creating holograms that were viewable using ordinary white light. However, Dr. Dennis Gabor at the Imperial College of London, is considered to be the inventor of what we now know as the full-fledged holography.

A hologram contains data about the size and shape as well as basic brightness and contrast of the subject. This information is stored in an intricate infinitesimal pattern of "interference." The interference pattern is possible because of the properties of laser light. The light reflected by a three dimensional object forms a very complicated pattern that is also three-dimensional. In order to record the whole pattern, the light used must be highly directional and must be of one color. This is called coherent light, and light from a laser fills the bill: it is one color and one frequency.

When a light is shone on a hologram at the proper angle, the information that is stored as an interference pattern takes the incoming light and recreates the original optical wave front that was reflected off the original object. This makes it look as if the object is in front of you once again.

Early holograms needed lasers in order to be viewed but

modern holograms can be seen with most available lighting. However, direct sunlight or a single overhead spotlight is the best way to illuminate holograms with deep imagery.

Embossed holograms, with shallower imagery, can be viewed with weaker lighting than full-fledged holograms. These are simpler holograms designed for commercial mass production. Very complex microscopic patterns are embossed onto rolls of very thin plastic or foil materials and light interacts with these patterns to create the holographic image.

The commercially available holograms include:

3D: These display a three dimensional image which looks identical to a solid object. The viewer can look around the top and sides of the image just like the actual object was there. Under proper illumination, images project right out of the hologram or appear to be behind it.

2D/3D: These holograms display a unique multi-level, multi-color effect. These images have one or two levels of flat graphics that seem to float above or at the surface of the hologram. Background artwork seems to be under or behind the hologram and this gives the illusion of depth. These can be viewed under a wide variety of light sources.

Stereograms: This is movie film that is processed holographically to create a multi-dimensional effect. Special effects, computer graphics, animated subjects, and even outdoor scenes can all be utilized but the dimensionality is extremely limited.

Real Image: If an image jumps right out of the hologram and appears in front of the film, it is "real," since it has left the "virtual" world inside the film and entered the "real" world.

Virtual Image: If an image appears to be on the other side of the hologram, or behind, like looking through a window, it is called "virtual." If you view it normally, right side out it is "orthoscopic." If the hologram is flipped, the image is inside out and is "pseudoscopic." Any combination of these effects is possible.

Obviously, the holographic equipment in the Xavier Mansion's Danger Room has many therapeutic uses besides the training of mutants in combat. Perhaps one day Professor X and the guys and gals will share this nifty alien technology with the rest of us.

BASEMENT

This is mostly a normal basement: It has oil and water heaters and is used for storage of furniture, books, and wine. It also contains the mansion's auxiliary generator, the main memory components of the mansion's computer system, and an entrance to a secret passageway which leads to the lower levels.

FIRST FLOOR

The main entrance is here, along with a back door that leads to the swimming pool and most of the rest of the estate.

There are more extensive intruder-alert surveillance and security systems on this floor than on the other floors and throughout the estate.

This level includes an impressively furnished living room, main dining room, a smaller, informal dining room for breakfast and lunch, and a sitting room, mainly for visitors to the school.

Additionally, there is a huge library, where the majority of the school's classes are held, the main computer room, and the kitchen facilities.

Here also are rooms reserved for Professor Xavier's sole usage: his study, where the principal terminal of his Cerebro device (see entry) is located, the office where he conducts school business, and his private dining quarters which also extend to the next floor.

SECOND FLOOR

Most of the students have their private quarters here. Xavier's bedroom is here and his quarters, which reach to the floor beneath.

There are two residential wings. There are also laundry facilities, a workshop, and a recreation area.

THE ATTIC

This is mostly used for general storage. There is, however, one sizeable segment adapted to residential use. Storm prefers this spacious attic room to the smaller rooms occupied by her fellow X-Men. Her quarters here contain her vast collection of plants which receive sunlight through the large skylight.

There is also a large "playroom" on this level that is used as a recreation area, a room for communications equipment, and the stairway up to the mansion's cupola.

THE CUPOLA

This is the only level of the mansion that is completely as it seems. It's just a nice cupola on top of the enormous building that lets the team members catch a little fresh air and look out over the rolling hills and the lake of the vast estate.

THE GROUNDS

Another Olympic-sized swimming pool is directly to the rear of the mansion. Elsewhere on the property there are stables, so the mutants can canter about the estate, and a boat-house, for recreational water sports on the lake.

SUBTERRANEAN TUNNELS AND HANGARS

High-speed magnetic rail cars travel from under the mansion through a tunnel to subterranean hangar buildings and a takeoff and landing pad—far from public view—for the X-Men's Blackbird jet (see Blackbird entry).

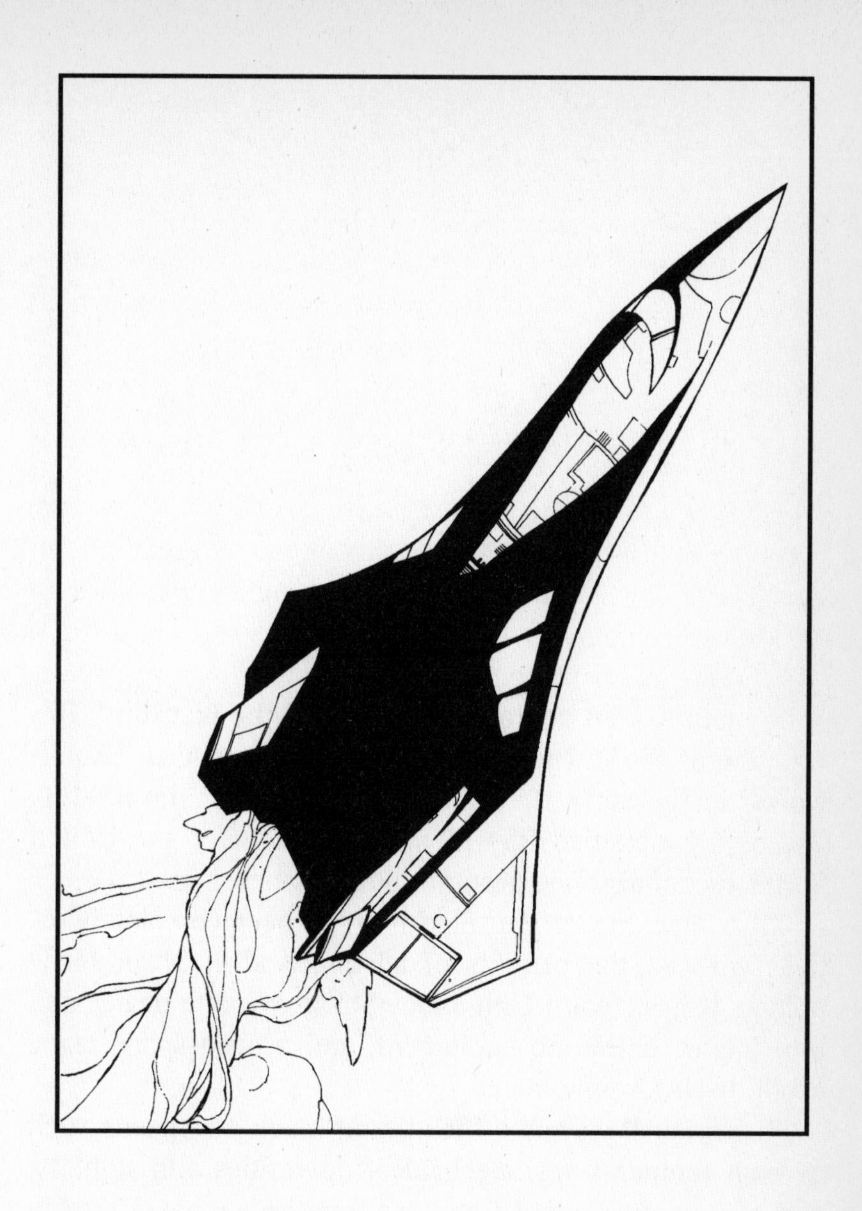

BLACKBIRD JET

The main X-Men aircraft is a jet called the Blackbird. This was one of the last jets designed by the Lockheed "Skunkworks" in the early 1970s and was designated the RS-150. The highly classified RS-150 was intended for the United States reconnaissance program but was never used.

Of course, the current Blackbird has been completely rebuilt with all the benefits of advanced alien Shi'ar technology. It has stealth technology Shi'ar cloaking device and intelligence gathering equipment, and a deep-space ready cabin. If NASA only knew!

The original jet had difficulties at Mach 4+ speeds, such as high temperatures, mechanical operations and stability, and routine equipment functions. These have been fixed in the new model.

The original Blackbird was designated the SR-71 and was code-named Oxcart during its development. It flies on a tremendous 65,000 lbs. of thrust at an altitude of 100,000+ feet at Mach 3.5, and has a range of four thousand miles. That's four times faster and seven miles higher than the U-2,

TECHNICAL DATA

	ORIGINAL BLACKBIRD SR-71	X-MEN'S BLACKBIRD RS-150
Construction	Titanium (Beta-120/Ti-13V-11Cr-3A1) Monococque with super-high-temperature plastics.	unknown
Length	107 feet, 5 inches	88'4"
Wingspan	55 feet, 7 inches	62'6"
Wing Area	1,795 square feet	
Height	16 feet, 6 inches	19'2"
Maximum Gross Takeoff Weight	140,000 pounds	Over 145,000 pounds

the previous high-altitude champion, for those of you keeping score.

For quite a while the Air Force claimed a maximum speed record of Mach 3.2 and an operational ceiling of 85,000 feet, but thanks to partial declassification of information we know that the SR-71 can soar above 100,000 feet. The SR-71 flew at least 60 percent faster than the recorded maximum speed on afterburner of the fastest jet fighter known in America at the time. Experimental rocket engines had flown this fast, but only for two or three minutes before running out of fuel. The Blackbird can cruise at more than three times the speed of sound, and fly coast-to-coast in less than an hour on one tank of gas. What's more, the aircraft can also survey more than 100,000 square miles of the Earth's surface in one hour. Because of the great temperatures experienced by its titanium hull, the Blackbird actually stretches a few inches during flight. It also suffers some minor instabilities at Mach 3 speed.

The Lockheed SR-71 was sent into retirement in 1990. It is surmised that it will be or has already been followed in development by the highly classified Aurora aircraft. The Aurora is rumored to be able to fly at Mach 6. Some say that its sonic booms have been recorded in the Nevada desert and it has been sighted off an oil platform in the UK's North Sea.

ALIEN RACES

It is only recently that astronomers, with the aid of the Hubble telescope, have been able to suggest that some of the other star systems out there have planets. That is just one of the myriad factors that must be in place for life like ours to evolve. A planet that promotes the evolution of biological processes must be a certain distance from the sun that water—a necessary prerequisite—will neither boil nor freeze. The planet must be heavy enough to hold an atmosphere but not so heavy as to crush delicate life form with immense gravitic and atmosphere pressures. A satellite moon might also be necessary to draw off some of the heavier elements of the evolving primordial atmosphere and then create tides that will expose marine life to open air and promote land life. The list goes on.

Of course, there is the less likely possibility that life could evolve in vastly different circumstances. We see no evidence of life on any of the planets or asteroids of our solar system so the evolution of life can't be that much of a universal process. But it's a big universe and that allows for a lot of outside chances. Additionally, we now know that life exists in the extreme environments of the Antarctic regions, the driest hottest deserts, and the deep sea. It did not evolve in those conditions, however. Or did it? Many deep sea marine biologists are looking with great interest at the life forms that live around deep-sea fissures-volcano-like openings into the molten interior of the Earth. These life-forms rely upon the heat of the boiling fissures for much of their biological energy. There is much speculation that the early environment of the Earth was much like this and that the earliest, most primitive life forms might have resembled what life still survives in the lowest depths of the planet's oceans.

When mankind finally manages to cross the incredible distances of interstellar space we might find independently evolved life. Maybe not on the first star we reach, nor the second or third. But perhaps in the thousandth star system we will find someone that can wave or wiggle a greeting back at us. It will be fascinating to see if all intelligent life has to follow the same rules of evolution that we did. Will they have two of everything life mammals or three like insects or five like starfish? Will they have two frontal lobes in their brains... or will they have anything that resemble our brains at all? Will they sleep at night? Will they have music, jokes, and television drama?

The X-Men have met many alien races and answered some of these questions. No doubt, in time they will meet many more races and answer more of the questions that all intelligent life forms must ponder.

SHI'AR

The Shi'ar are an ancient alien race with advanced technology. They evolved from bird-like creatures—some of them have wings—and are the main race of a huge empire in another galaxy.

The Shi'ar are basically a peaceful race but at times they have conquered other races to incorporate them into their empire. This approach has been ameliorated somewhat since the deposition of their mad Emperor D'Ken.

A religiously observant race, the Shi'ar follow the example of their chief gods, Sharra and K'ythri. This couple was forced into a marriage which made them stronger. Therefore, the Shi'ar seek out other cultures to "marry" into their own as they believe this strengthens their Empire.

The leader of the Shi'ar empire—the Majestrix—is Lilandra Neramani, who is wingless, unlike her sister, Ca'Syee Neramani, also known as Deathbird. Her other royal relatives include the late Emperor (her brother) D'Ken, Deathbird's son Black Light, Deathbird's daughter White Noise, and the character X-Treme who might possibly be her nephew Neramani, son of D'Ken.

CONVERGENT EVOLUTION

The Shi'ar could be considered to be an example of convergent evolution. Their distant ancestors were bird-like animals while ours resembled shrews. Apparently, the Shi'ar evolved to fit the same evolutionary niche in their world as do humans on Earth.

This could be seen as analogous to the case of the Australian marsupials who fit the same ecological niches as do dogs and cats in the West.

One indication of this convergent evolution is that we've seen a tendency for intelligent species to evolve the same set of physiological tools: opposable thumbs, upright posture, stereographic vision, and so on.

Perhaps any species, given the necessary brain size and structure—including the capacity for learning and the prerequisite ability to avoid predators—is capable of evolving toward intelligence. Certainly, birds seem like prime candidates. They are bipeds, have color stereographic vision, and recent experiments have shown they can be trained to speak with limited vocabularies. The work of Irene Pepperberg has proved that gray parrots, for example, can be trained to ask questions, solve simple logical problems, and even understand the concept of zero.

Are the Shi'ar truly bird-like? It's difficult to answer that question in that they are aliens and have evolved on another planet. It's certainly tempting to consider the possibility.

CULTURAL TECHNOLOGICAL SUPERIORITY

It has been a general supposition of our cultural anthropologists that as a culture advances it trims down its pantheon of gods until it arrives at monotheism. This observation is largely based on the role of the Judeo-Christian tradition in Western culture.

Evidently the Shi'ar have a different cultural dynamic, as they retain worship of many gods and have not one central god but two. Among human cultures, this would be equated with a non-technological culture, in the early Iron Age stage of development.

Obviously, the Shi'ar are not human, but they are humanoid in appearance and behave as humans in almost every respect. Despite their technological superiority, they maintain a religious/superstitious belief system that in human anthropological studies is equated with non-technological, primitive cultures. Does this mean that they are a de-evolved culture, preserving technology from a more advanced period in their history, but culturally they are little more than savages? Perhaps. But it's unwise to judge strangers by our own anthropological standards. What if the Shi'ar fabulous technology was not an indigenous development but, rather a grafted one: perhaps they inherited it from a more advanced race.

BROOD

The Brood are an intelligent alien race-although sometimes their actions seem to belie that. They are insect-like but have rows of shark-like, razor-sharp teeth. Their size varies but they are generally larger than humans. Like bees, they have a hive-centered social structure that revolves around a queen. Like ants, they have warriors and drones. There are also elite corps of armored assassins who serve and protect the queen. These sometimes have teleportation abilities.

The Brood use what they consider to be genetically superior alien life-forms as hosts for their eggs. When a brood of Brood hatches it takes over its host's form for an extended time period. It can assume its true Brood appearance but can only resume its host's form while some of the host's persona remains. During that time, the hatchling can use any powers the host might have had.

WEARING SKELETONS ON THE OUTSIDE

Insects wear their skeletons on the outside of their bodies as exoskeletons. These rigid carapaces are made of chitin, an organic compound that is softer than the internal bone skeletons of mammals, marsupials, birds, and fish. Chitin is primarily composed of an insoluble nitrogenous polysaccharide while bones are made of the mineral calcium. (The shells of shellfish are made of a similar chitin-like compound.)

A human-sized insect like the Brood would most likely collapse under its own weight as chitin could not support it. This must then be a case of convergent evolution. Although the Brood look like insects it is only because they fill the same ecological niche in their own ecosystem. Their exoskeletons are not actually made of chitin but from a much harder substance that supports their internal organs under various gravitational conditions.

The Brood are an extreme example of parasites, a species that lives on or in another life-form which it draws nourishment, in the process of which the host is destroyed. This aggressive species seeks out aliens whom they consider to be genetically superior life forms to use as hosts for their eggs.

This is one example of their bizarrely irrational thinking that seems to contradict other indications of sapience. After all, there is no such thing as genetic superiority. One might say that humans have more genes and more complex arrangements of genes, but the genes themselves are just genes.

From the complexity of the Brood life functions, it is obvious that their genetic structure is at least as large and complex as human structures. Their avarice toward appropriating human DNA seems baseless. Perhaps they have an atavistic urge from an earlier stage of evolution but their intelligence should enable them to override that, just as we are able to override our urges to breed without limits, to steal whatever we wanted, and to fight any opposing group. Perhaps their instinctive urges, unlike ours, are impossible to override.

BIBLIOGRAPHY

American Society for Psychical Research (http://www.aspr.com/).

Asimov, Isaac. *Please Explain*, (Houghton Mifflin, 1973).

Brown, Julian. "A Quantum Revolution for Computing," *New Scientist*, September-1994.

Cohen, David W. *An Introduction to Hilbert Space and Quantum Logic*, Springer-Verlag New York Inc., 1989.

Deutsch, David. "Quantum Theory as a Universal Physical Theory," *International Journal of Theoretical Physics*, Vol 24 #1 1985.

Deutsch, David. *Three Connections between Everett's Interpretation and Experiment*, Oxford University Press 1986.

DeWitt, Bryce S. "Quantum Mechanics and Reality," *Physics Today*, Vol 23 #9 30–40 September 1970.

Encyclopedia Britannica online (http://www.eb.com/).

Everett III, Hugh. " 'Relative State' Formulation of Quantum Mechanics," reviews of *Modern Physics* Vol 29 #3 454–462, July 1957.

Everett III, Hugh. "Formulation of Quantum Mechanics," reviews of *Modern Physics*, Vol 29 #3 454–462, July 1957.

Everett III, Hugh. "The Theory of the Universal Wavefunction," Princeton thesis 1956.

Feinberg, Gerald. "Physics and Life Prolongation," *Physics Today* Vol 19 #11 45 1966.

Fermi, Enrico. *Course IL: Foundations of Quantum Mechanics*, Bryce S DeWitt, R Neill Graham eds. (Academic Press, 1972).

Feynman, Richard P., Leighton, Robert & Sands, Matthew. *The Feynman Lectures on Physics*, Addison Wesley Longman, Inc., 1990.

Foward, Robt L. *Indistinguishable from Magic*, Baen, 1995.

Gell-Mann, Murray & Hartle, James B. "The Duality in Matter and Light," *Scientific American*, December 1994).

Giancoli, Douglas C. *The Ideas of Physics*, Harcourt Brace Jovanovich, 1986.

Goldstein, Martin & Inge. *The Refrigerator and the Universe: Understanding the Laws of Energy*, Harvard University Press, 1993.

Gribbin, John & Chimsky, Mark. *Schrodinger's Kittens: And the Search for Reality*, Little, Brown & Company, March 1996.

Gribbin, John & Mary eds. *Q Is for Quantum: An Encyclopedia of Particle Physics*, Simon & Schuster Trade, 2000.

Gribbin, John. *In Search of Schrödinger's Cat*, Bantam Books, Toronto: 1984.

Gribbin, John. *In Search of the Big Bang: The Life and Death of the Universe*, Viking Penguin, 1999.

Gribbin, John. *In Search of the Edge of Time: Black Holes, White Holes, Wormholes*, Viking Penguin, 1999.

Gribbin, John. *The Search for Superstrings, Symmetry and the Theory of Everything*, Little, Brown & Company, 1998.

Gruenwald, Mark, Editor. *The Official Handbook of the Marvel Universe* Volumes 1–10, Marvel Comics Group, 1986–1987.

Hawking, Stephen & Penrose, Roger. *The Nature of Space*

and Time Isaac Newton Institute Series of Lectures, Princeton University Press, 1996.

Hawking, Stephen. *A Brief History of Time*, Bantam Doubleday Dell Pub, 1980.

Hilbert, David and S. Cohn-Vossen, *Geometry and the Imagination*, American Mathematical Society, 1952.

Hofstadter, Douglas. *Godel Escher Bach*, Bantam New Age Books, 1981.

Hofstadter, Douglas. *The Mind's Eye*, Bantam New Age Books, 1980.

Human Genome Project web site (http://www.ornl.gov/hgmis).

Inspector General. *Report on the CIA MK Ultra, 1963, U.S. Gov't., 1963.*

Jammer, Max. *The Philosophy of Quantum Mechanics*, Wiley, New York 1974.

Luminet, Jean-Pierre, Starkman, Glenn D. & Jeffrey R. Weeks. "Is Space Finite?" *Scientific American*, April 1999.

Macaulay, David. *The Way Things Work*, (Houghton Mifflin 1988).

McSween, Jr., Harry. *Stardust to Planets—A Geological Tour of the Universe*, St. Martin's Griffin, 1993.

New York Times online, Science and Circuits sections (http://www.nytimes.com/).

Penrose, Roger. *The Emperor's New Mind*, Oxford 1990.

Pepperberg, Irene Maxine. *Cognitive and Communicative Abilities of Grey Parrots*, Harvard University Press, 2000.

Rae, Alastair. *Quantum Physics: Illusion or Reality?* Cambridge University Press, London: 1986.

ScienceNow, the daily news web site of *Science Magazine* (http://www.sciencenow.org/).

Silver & Rosenbluth, eds., *The Handbook of Borderline Personality Disorders*, International Universities Press, 1992.

Times/Hammond. *Concise Atlas of World History*, Times/Hammond, 1986.

Tipler, Frank J. "The Many-Worlds Interpretation of Quantum Mechanics in Quantum Cosmology" in *Quantum Concepts of Space and Time* eds. Roger Penrose and Chris Isham, Oxford University Press 1986.

Tudge, Colin. *The Time Before History*, Scribner, 1996.

Van Loon, Hendrick. *The Story of Mankind*, Garden City, 1921.

Wheeler, John A. & Zurek, Wojciech H. eds. *Quantum Theory and Measurement*, Princeton Series in Physics. Princeton University Press 1983.

Wheeler, John A. "Assessment of Everett's,. 'Relative State' Formulation of Quantum Theory," reviews of *Modern Physics* Vol 29 #3 463–465 July 1957.

Wolke, Robert. *What Einstein Didn't know, DTP, 1997.*

Zurek, Wojciech H. "Decoherence and the Transition from the Quantum to the Classical," *Physics Today*, 36–44 October 1991.

Zurek, Wojciech H. "Preferred States, Predictability, Classicality, and the Environment-Induced Decoherence," *Progress of Theoretical Physics*, Vol 89 #2 281–312 1993.